Doug Johnstone is the author of three novels, most recently *Smokeheads* (2011), described in *The Times* as 'a hugely atmospheric thriller soaked in the spirit of life'. Writer-in-residence at the University of Strathclyde, he is also a free-lance journalist, a songwriter and musician, and has a PhD in nuclear physics. He lives in Edinbur

dougjohnstone.word
dougjohnstone.band<

D1151693

Praise for *Smokeheads*:

'It lulls the reader with the warm glow of a good dram on a winter's night, then ambushes him with all the bitter nasti-ness of a brutal whisky hangover.' Christopher Brookmyre

'It will have you laughing and wincing in equal measure as – thanks to the passion with which Johnstone writes about his main subject – you are left punch-drunk by the whisky fumes that rise from the page.' *Guardian*

'It is so well written . . . there is plenty of flesh and blood here, much of it splashing across the page.' *Scotsman*

'It's unlikely you'll find a novel with the same rocketing pace . . . All the fun of a wild weekend without the hangover.' *Financial Times*

'*Smokeheads* has a lingering sense of melancholy – as well as some brutal scenes. The two moods, sadness and savagery, meet in a plot that swiftly hooks the reader. It's measured out in short chapters, which, like a good nip, go down fast and deliver a jolt.' *Herald*

'A major discovery this year for crime cultists . . . intense . . . insightful . . . fresh.' spinetinglermag.com

---

By the Same Author
Tombstoning
The Ossians
Smokeheads

Hit and Run

DOUG JOHNSTONE

ff

faber and faber

First published in 2012
by Faber and Faber Limited
Bloomsbury House
74–77 Great Russell Street
London WC1B 3DA

This paperback edition first published in 2012

Typeset by Faber and Faber Limited

Printed and bound by CPI Group (UK) Ltd, Croydon CR0 4YY

A CIP record for this book
is available from the British Library

ISBN 978-0-571-27047-7

4 6 8 10 9 7 5

For Trish, always

Acknowledgements

Immeasurable thanks to Trish, Allan Guthrie, Angus Cargill, Katherine Armstrong, Alex Holroyd, Sam Brown, John McColgan, Lisa Baker and everyone else at Faber.

The writer gratefully acknowledges support from Creative Scotland towards the writing of this book.

They shouldn't have been going this way. Billy wasn't even sure where they were. He definitely shouldn't have been driving. He'd lost count of the number of beetroot schnapps he'd downed. That was the problem with free drink. And the pills Charlie gave them. What were they again? Charlie liked to throw medical names around to seem clever – Zetran, Pervitin, Oramorph. They sounded like aliens from an obscure sci-fi movie.

Whatever the pills were, they were kicking in now. He felt a rush, his eyeballs throbbing, pulse hard in his throat. The tips of his fingers on the steering wheel tingled like after a snowball fight. The left side of his face was numb. He glanced at Zoe in the passenger seat. Beautiful, cool Zoe. Black fringe, pale skin, hippie-chic dress. She reached over and squeezed his thigh and it felt like her fingers were moulding the clay of his leg, squeezing down to the bone beneath.

He tried to concentrate on driving. Where the hell were they? Which way was home? It wasn't easy to focus with Charlie yammering away in the back.

'Beetroot schnapps, honest to fuck.' Charlie slapped the back of Billy's seat.

'I know,' Zoe said, shaking her head. 'Awful.'

Billy belched and tasted rancid earthiness in his mouth. He pictured the blood-red shot glasses clustered on trays, sexy Aryan models handing them out. Some expensive re-branding of an Austrian peasant drink in an ultra-cool warehouse in Leith. It was nuts the freebies Zoe got through her work.

They never usually went out in Leith, they were Southside these days. They'd staggered out of the glass and concrete box fifteen minutes ago and looked at the wasteland around them. They were lost. The guy on the door warned them police were doing random drink-drive stops on Leith Walk and the Bridges, and they should go a different way.

How had Billy ended up behind the wheel? He looked round the car. Zoe's head was wobbling and her eyelids flickered. Charlie was blethering loudly to himself, smacking the roof of the Micra to emphasise his point. His thick arms were tense and his eyes wild.

Billy saw a roundabout ahead and crunched the gears.

'Hey, watch Mum's car, Bro.' Charlie ruffled Billy's hair. Billy hated it when he did that. They still called it Mum's car, even though she'd been dead five years.

He took the roundabout too fast, swerving in an arc then heading straight on, jostling them all in their seats. They drove past a pond. He realised where they were. A ruined chapel loomed over them on the left, the well-manicured lawn of Holyrood Park on the other side. They'd be home in a few minutes. Up Queen's Drive, hang a couple of rights past the Commie Pool and they'd be in Rankeillor Street in no time.

The dashboard clock said 2.37 a.m. The streets were empty. Edinburgh in July, the majority of students had fucked off and the festival pricks were yet to arrive.

Charlie's fist thudded on his shoulder as they approached another roundabout.

'Hey, Bro, when are you gonna start getting sweet freebies like your lady here?'

Charlie had already mentioned this several times tonight in the warehouse bar. Either he didn't remember or he didn't give a shit and was just on the wind-up.

'Well?'

Billy felt like sighing but laughed instead. Must be the chemicals slewing through his blood cells and synapses.

'Crime reporting isn't the heady heights of lifestyle journalism.' Billy couldn't help himself, his voice made sarcastic quote marks around the last two words.

'Hey.' Zoe swayed round to punch him on the arm. 'I didn't see you refusing any beetroot schnapps earlier.'

'Yeah, or my fucking pills,' Charlie said.

Another freebie, somehow liberated from the ERI where Charlie worked.

Billy shook his head. 'The only freebie I'm likely to get is an invite to a crime scene.'

'That would be cool,' Charlie shouted, bouncing in the back seat. He put on a thick accent. 'There's been a murder.'

Since Billy started a month ago, it had been constant jibes about *Taggart* and *Rebus*. The truth of trainee crime reporting so far was astonishingly mundane, but Billy liked the methodical clarity of the work, trying to create order from the mess of real life.

They were climbing a slope now, Salisbury Crags towering on the left, trees lining the road on the other side. It felt like the countryside. Houses and shops and pubs were two minutes away, but it seemed like the middle of nowhere.

'Hey, check out the stars,' Charlie said, leaning forward.

'Hey, check out the stars,' Zoe repeated in a stoner voice.

Charlie laughed. 'Fuck you, droopy drawers.'

'Fuck you right back.' Zoe threw him a flirty look.

Billy felt a rush of chemical love for his girlfriend and brother, the drugs thrusting his feelings into the stratosphere. They were a regular Three Musketeers, one for all, and all for one.

Zoe craned her neck to look through the windscreen. 'Actually, that is kind of beautiful.'

Billy laughed. 'Jesus, what was in those pills?'

'Better if you don't know,' Charlie said. He liked to be secretive about the drugs he pilfered from A&E cabinets, but Billy trusted him. Charlie was his big brother after all, the one person supposed to look after him. Charlie wouldn't let him come to any harm.

Anyway, the pills they took were pretty predictable. Uppers to get the night going, opiates, benzodiazepines or barbiturates to come down. Judging by the buzz, they were on something speedy, maybe MDMA as well. Methamphetamine and mephedrone?

Charlie was looking out his passenger window now, trees

blurring past, his face pointing up. 'Seriously, that sky is fucking amazing. You gotta check it out, Bro.'

Zoe laughed and looked at Billy and he smiled back at her. The road bent round in a slow curve as they climbed the hill. Billy leaned forward so his chin was almost touching the steering wheel and gazed upwards.

The moon hung there, surrounded by a whirl of stars, needles of light puncturing the deep violet sky. The Crags to their left were like a rocket launch pad jutting into the expanse of glimmering life.

Billy turned his head to look the other way. There was an almighty jolt in the car and a monstrous crashing noise, something solid and heavy smashing into metal and glass, followed by a ripple of sound across their roof and the weighty thunk of whatever it was landing on the road behind them.

Billy lunged for the brake. His left temple cracked against the windscreen and his chest pressed into the steering wheel. The car glided for a moment, its nose pointing towards an embankment and a small copse of trees, then it righted itself in a screech of brakes and the crunch of tyres on tarmac. The car lurched to a stop and Billy was thudded into his seat as the engine stalled.

The smell of burning brake pads and rubber. The tick and creak of the engine.

Billy felt a bursting pain above his left eye, and a deeper, pulsing ache through his neck and shoulders. His fingers and toes were fizzing. He rubbed his temple and felt a thick lump under the skin. He cricked his neck and a blade of pain shot through his upper body.

He looked round. Zoe had both hands pressed against the dashboard, her eyes closed.

'You OK?' he said.

She nodded.

He tried to clear his head. He removed Zoe's hands from the dashboard and felt her body relax a little. She turned to him, her eyes slits.

'You sure you're all right?'

She nodded again.

Billy turned to the back of the car, his neck aching. Charlie was sprawled across the seats. No seat belt on. Lucky he hadn't been sitting forward. He was righting himself in a flustered mess of limbs.

'I'm fucking fine,' he said, irritated. He rubbed his arm. 'What the fuck happened?'

'We hit something.' Billy looked through the back windscreen at the curve of road behind them.

'No shit.' Charlie followed Billy's gaze. 'What was it?'

'I don't know.'

Billy opened his door and eased out, his body stiff, his legs shaky. He walked to the rear of the car. He heard the click and clunk of car doors as Charlie and Zoe followed.

In the red glow of the Micra's tail lights, he could see something on the road a few yards away. He walked unsteadily towards it.

'Christ.' He rubbed the lump on his temple. His hands shook and he felt his breath shorten. He inched forward until he was standing over the body. It was face down, torso twisted sideways, legs splayed out. It was a man, middle-aged, in a suit and tie. Short hair.

'Mate?' Billy's voice was quivering and high. 'Are you all right?'

Charlie was next to him now. 'Is he alive?'

Billy looked at his brother. 'You're the doctor.'

Charlie knelt down and took the man's wrist. Billy could hear the faint sound of traffic in the distance, over the embankment. He could see right down to Holyrood Park, just wildlife and darkness. The stars still sparkled overhead.

'I'm not getting anything,' Charlie said.

He turned the body over. The face was a bloody mess, a sticky pool of dark red left on the road.

'Fucking hell,' Billy said.

Charlie put two fingers to the man's neck and waited a few moments.

Billy was aware of Zoe next to him, her body rigid.

Charlie sighed. 'He's dead.'

'Shit,' Zoe said, and took Billy's hand.

Billy pulled away. His chest tightened. He struggled to breathe. The lump on his head pounded pain through his body. He pulled his mobile out.

Charlie stood up. 'Wait a minute, what are you doing?'

Billy pressed 999. 'What do you think I'm doing?'

'Let's think about this.'

'What is there to think about?'

Billy pressed 'call'. Charlie strode towards him and grappled the phone from his hand. Billy didn't resist too

7

hard. Charlie was shorter but stronger, more determined. You couldn't win a fight with Charlie.

Charlie pressed 'end call' and waved the phone at Billy. 'You want to ruin our lives? Is that what you want?'

'But . . .'

'He's dead, there's nothing we can do.'

'But we have to report it.' Billy's voice was straining.

'We're all drunk. And loaded on stolen medical supplies. You were driving. It'll kill our careers, wreck our lives. Is that what Mum would've wanted?'

Billy felt tears spring to his eyes. He couldn't think straight.

'Charlie's right,' Zoe said.

Billy had forgotten she was there. He turned. He couldn't work out the look in her eyes. She had a hand out, reaching for him, pleading. He wanted to grab her and hold her until this all went away.

'There's no point making things any worse,' she said. 'It was an accident. He came out of nowhere. None of us saw him.'

Billy looked round, his heart hammering against his ribcage. 'So we just drive off? Is that what you're saying?'

A faint noise made them turn. Down the hill in the distance, two headlights were reaching out along Queen's Drive. The growl of a diesel engine. A taxi. Still a long way away. There was a chance it might turn right at the roundabout, head past the *Standard* offices instead of up the hill.

'Shit,' Charlie said.

He turned to the other two. 'Zoe, kill the lights. Billy, come here.'

They both stood still, staring at the headlights in the distance.

'Do it,' he shouted, making them jump. Zoe ran to the car as Charlie pulled his brother staggering towards the body.

'Get his legs.'

Billy held the man's ankles. Expensive leather shoes, scuffed now. He felt Charlie lift the man's arms.

Charlie pointed at the small clump of trees to the side of the road. 'That way.'

Billy shuffled backwards with the ankles in his grip, almost dropping them. The man's arse scraped on the tarmac between them.

They were plunged into near darkness as Zoe reached the car and switched the lights off. She removed the key and slammed the door, then headed over to them.

Charlie and Billy looked the other way. The taxi went straight on at the roundabout, heading up the hill towards them. Still some distance, headlights pointing away, thanks to the bend in the road.

They struggled to the pavement with the body, the headlights creeping round the opposite embankment towards them. Zoe took an ankle from Billy as they lugged the body. They reached the edge of the slope and heaved the corpse down into the trees and thick foliage.

The taxi was almost on them now, chugging up the hill. Charlie and Zoe grabbed Billy and shoved him down the embankment, diving after him.

Billy landed in thick nettles, stinging his hands, his face only a few inches from the dead man. Charlie landed next to him with a thump, Zoe rolling on top of Charlie in the mayhem.

They heard the taxi engine ease off as the driver spotted the parked car and slowed. Then the revs picked up as he sped past the Micra and disappeared up the hill.

The fading engine rumble left a vacuum behind. All Billy could hear was his own heavy breathing and a thin rustling of leaves. Zoe extricated herself from Charlie then the two of them got up. Billy didn't look at the dead body, only a few inches away to his right. Instead he gazed up at the sky packed full of stars.

Zoe and Charlie offered him their hands, and he let himself be lifted. Every movement meant more nettle stings, but Billy somehow enjoyed the sharp jabs of pain.

They scrambled up the bank, Zoe and Charlie ahead of him. Billy looked along the road. Darkness in both directions.

'Come on,' Charlie said. He pushed Billy into the back seat of the Micra then took the keys from Zoe. 'I'll drive.'

He got in the driving seat, Zoe in the front passenger seat. Billy alone in the back. Charlie started the engine and switched the lights on, then pulled out sharply, forcing Billy into his seat. As they drove away, he stared out the window at the starry sky, his mind numb.

2

Charlie opened the front door.

'I need a fucking drink.'

Billy felt Zoe's hand on his back, nudging him forward. He stumbled into the flat. Charlie was already heading downstairs to the basement kitchen and they followed like zombies.

Charlie set out three long tumblers and half-filled each with vodka from the freezer. He handed them out.

'Here.'

The three of them stood around the breakfast table. The spotlighting made it look like they were hatching a plot. Billy stared at the liquid in his glass then looked at Charlie, who had downed his already and was refilling it.

'We did the right thing,' Charlie said.

'Did we?' Billy stared back at his glass.

Charlie took Billy's glass from him and set it on the table. He pulled a chair out. 'Sit down.'

Billy sat. Zoe took the chair next to him, Charlie across the table. Their three glasses made sweat marks on the scuffed pine.

'We didn't have any choice,' Charlie said. 'There's nothing we could've done for him.'

'We should've reported it,' Billy said.

Charlie took Billy's hand across the table. 'Look at me.'

Billy lifted his head. His brother's eyes were cold.

'What would've happened if we'd called the police?'

Billy didn't speak.

'What would've happened?'

Billy shook his head.

'We would all have been arrested. Breathalysed. Drug tests. Prison. No jobs, no future. Criminal records. You would've got it worst, you were driving.'

Zoe took Billy's other hand. 'Charlie's right. I don't like this any more than you do, but reporting it wouldn't have made any difference.'

Holding hands like this felt like they were holding a seance.

'Think about Mum,' Charlie said.

The mention of her made Billy snatch his hands from theirs and reach for his glass. The cold tumbler felt good against his nettle-stung hands. He downed the vodka, a viscous burn in his throat and chest. Almost five years. A massive stroke, she never regained consciousness. Him and Charlie still kids really, early days at Uni, only each other to cling to.

'Don't bring her into it.'

'She always wanted to be proud of us, and she would be. I'm a doctor, you've just landed a proper job. Want to throw that away because of a stupid accident?'

Charlie topped their glasses up. Billy grabbed his and gulped. He lowered his glass and stared at Charlie.

'Do you actually think we'll get away with it?'

Charlie held his gaze and shrugged. 'Why not?'

'What about the taxi driver?'

'What about him?'

'He saw the car.'

'He won't have been paying attention. It was just a car parked at night. And it's dark. Even if he did notice anything, there must be hundreds of red Micras in this city.'

Billy shook his head. Zoe reached out and gently stroked his hair, lifting it up at the hairline over his temple.

'How's your head?' she said.

Billy reached up and touched her hand, their interlocked fingers playing over the bump. It felt like an alien egg implanted in his skull.

Charlie went to the freezer and took out an ice tray. He popped the cubes into a tea towel, folded it up then smashed it against the worktop, crushing the ice inside. He pulled it tight then put it against Billy's temple and placed Billy's hand on it.

'Keep that there as long as you can.'

The cold of it stung, sending shivers of pain across his head and down his neck. He realised one side of his face was still numb and began prodding it with his other hand, kneading the flesh. All the while, an itchy pain sparkled across his hands from the nettle stings.

Zoe rubbed his shoulder. 'Are you OK?'

He jerked away from her touch. 'Sore neck.' He tried to crick it.

'Probably whiplash,' Charlie said.

He dug into his pocket and came out with a handful of

blister packs. He sorted through them on the table, picking up one with MXL on it. He pushed out two large orange capsules and slid them across the table.

'Take these.'

'What are they?'

'Painkillers.'

'What kind?'

'Good ones. Just take them.'

Billy took the capsules and swigged them down with vodka.

Charlie sifted through the blister packs on the table and lifted one with Sonata printed on it. He popped half a dozen lime-green pills out on the table, split them into twos and pushed the pairs in front of each of them.

'These will help us sleep,' he said.

He took his, as did Zoe. Billy felt a bolt of icy pain come from the compress on his head. He looked at them both. He felt Zoe's hand on his leg, trying to be comforting. He remembered her touching him the same way in the car earlier.

He lifted his capsules, put them on his tongue, and washed them down with vodka. He sat back and waited to feel something.

*

'Hold me,' Zoe whispered.

They were in bed, almost dawn outside, thin light bleeding through the curtains.

She nestled into him as he lay on his back and stared at the cornicing. She lifted a leg across Billy's, brushing his crotch, then ran her hand up the inside of his thigh to his boxers.

'I want you inside me.' She kissed his ear. 'Forget everything and come inside me.'

She went to pull his shorts off but he put a hand on hers.

'Don't.' He looked at her and saw that she was scared too. 'It's the pills, I can't.'

She lifted her hand to his chest and snuggled in. 'Don't worry, baby. Just hold me.'

He lay for a few minutes until he heard her breath deepen and slow, then he slid out from her embrace and crept downstairs to the bathroom. He took out Charlie's *FHM* from the cupboard under the sink and sat on the toilet. He flicked through the pages for a while then dropped the magazine on the floor. He put his head in his hands and began to sob.

3

Something was trying to drag him out of a sleep hole. His phone. His phone was ringing.

He opened gummy eyes. He was sitting in the old chair in the corner of the bedroom in his shorts. The room was warm already, sunlight in spears through the gaps in the curtains. He scrunched his eyes and blinked a few times, getting used to the light.

His head and neck throbbed, the skin on his hands was puckered and red. He felt his temple. The bump had shrunk but hardened. He found his jeans and took his phone from the pocket. It said 'Rose' on the screen. He pressed answer.

'Now before you say anything, Kiddo, I know you're not supposed to be in today, but we've got a belter of a tip-off, and I thought you'd want to see some real-life reporting for once, instead of just rewriting boring press releases.'

'Morning, Rose,' Billy said.

'Jesus H, you sound rough as a badger's arse. Big night last night?'

'Something like that.'

'You kids and your parties. I remember the days. Go for it. At your age you bounce back like knicker elastic. Anyway, like I was saying, we've got a potential scoop on our hands. Want in?'

'What's the story?'

'Suspected suicide. Word on the street is that it might be someone already known to the police, as they say.'

'Yeah?'

'Just come meet me. It's on our frigging doorstep, so we've got a start on those tabloid pricks for once. The body was found this morning at the bottom of Salisbury Crags.'

'What?'

'You heard me, Kiddo. Got a jumper. Or maybe something a little more interesting, my sources tell me.'

'Salisbury Crags?'

'You're taking a while to wake up, eh?' She put on a voice as if talking to a toddler. 'Yes. Salisbury Crags. Why don't you extricate yourself from Little Miss Sunday Supplement, sling on your outsized trousers and meet me there in ten minutes?'

'I don't think . . .'

Rose's voice turned serious. 'I know this is strictly my shift, and you're supposed to be having some well-earned kip, but trust me, if you want to get on at this game and learn the ropes properly, you'll help me on this one.'

Billy hesitated. He looked at Zoe, still crashed out on sedatives. 'OK.'

'Good laddie, see you there.'

'Wait, where is it exactly?'

'Can't miss it, Kiddo, the place will be crawling with police. Look out for large swathes of crime-scene tape.'

'Right.'

Billy ended the call. A jumper at Salisbury Crags, just a few minutes' walk from their accident.

He stared at Zoe, thighs white against black lace panties, arms covering her breasts. He reached over and stroked a strand of hair away from her eyes. She looked peaceful.

He pulled on his clothes, his body aching. He left the room and padded along the hall to Charlie's door. He pushed it open. Charlie was spreadeagled naked on top of his covers, his room the usual mess of gadgets, magazines and junk. He was snoring heavily. Billy found his jacket and went through the pockets. He found two MXL blister packs, lifted them and tiptoed out of the room.

*

The sunlight made him cringe as he stepped out of the front door. A hot day, the air choked with traffic fumes and pollen, making him sneeze. He stopped when he reached the gate. Right in front of the house was the red Micra, parked as if nothing had happened.

He examined it. Ran a finger along the side panel, then the bumper and the bonnet. It was filthy, his finger came away grey and gritty. There didn't appear to be any damage, how could that be? Now that he looked closely, he could see a slight bevel in the bonnet, a little to the left of centre, and a corresponding dent in the bumper. Hardly even noticeable. In the reflecting sunshine he spotted a few indentations in the roof, small dimples in the curve of the metal. Jesus, was that it?

He looked at their heavy front door, the flat that Zoe's dad had bought for her when she started Uni, Billy and Charlie freeloading as usual. Further along the road at the end of Rankeillor Street was St Leonard's police station, an anonymous modern brick block. Beyond that loomed the ragged brown cliff of Salisbury Crags, buttressed by the near-vertical slope beneath, spreads of rough yellow gorse clinging on for dear life.

4

He turned the corner at the top of Queen's Drive. It all looked so different in the thick, shimmering sunlight. The expanse of gorse on the Crags seemed to glow. His head throbbed. The cliffs above looked less ominous than last night, just a mottled strip of rock against pale sky.

Cars zipped up and down Queen's Drive as normal. Two police cars and a van were parked on the large spread of grass to the right of the road, where the slope of Salisbury Crags levelled off and the gorse petered out. A rough square of police tape cordoned off an area of grass and gorse, half a dozen men in uniform or white overalls milling about.

It wasn't the scene of Billy's accident. That was at least two hundred yards away.

He looked from the crime scene back to the small clump of trees that lined the road. Where they'd left the body. What the fuck was going on? Was the body still in there?

He saw Rose puffing up the hill towards the crime scene. He dry-swallowed two of Charlie's capsules and went to meet her, the pills haunting his throat. She waved when she spotted him. She had a fag in her mouth and a huge suede shoulder bag. She was fifty, busty, divorced and coughing her lungs up when he met her a few yards from the police tape.

'Hey, Kiddo.' She was gasping, getting her breath back. 'You look as bad as I feel.'

Billy stroked the bump on his head then stole a glimpse at the copse of trees from this angle. Just a tight cluster of beech, cars swishing past alongside, nothing to see.

Rose began walking in the opposite direction towards the cordoned-off area. 'Come on, let's find a story.'

Billy traipsed after her. She was surprisingly fast. By the time he reached the crime scene, she was already talking to a middle-aged police officer with a neat grey beard and a smart suit. She had her notebook out and was making shorthand scribbles.

'Stuart, this is Billy, my toyboy,' she said. 'Billy, this is Detective Inspector Price. Or Stuart, if you know him like I do.'

DI Price put on a smile but didn't offer a hand. He turned back to Rose.

'As I was saying, the body was found at 9.15 this morning by a local woman walking her dog.'

'Name and address?' Rose raised her eyebrows.

Price smiled. 'I'll get it from one of the grunts in a minute. Anyway, the body was found in amongst the gorse bushes here, which would seem to indicate a suicide or a tragic accident up on the Radical Road.'

'Where?' Billy said.

Price pointed upwards. 'It's the name of the path that runs along the base of the cliffs, at the top of this slope.'

Billy shielded his eyes as he looked up. He'd lived in Edinburgh his whole life and never heard the name before.

'Got an ID on the deceased yet?' Rose said.

Price smiled and looked at her notebook. 'Not officially.'

She stopped writing and lowered the pad. It was like they were flirting.

'Go on,' she said.

'Officially he's a white male in his forties, average height and solid build, well dressed.'

Billy thought about last night.

'And unofficially?' Rose was giving him big eyes.

'It's Frank Whitehouse.' Price had a note of triumph in his voice.

'You're shitting me.'

'Absolutely not.'

'Holy crap, Frank Whitehouse.'

'Who?' Billy said.

Price turned to him. 'You're a crime reporter and you don't know who Frank Whitehouse is?'

'He's new,' Rose said. 'Learning the ropes.'

She turned to Billy. 'Frank Whitehouse is, or was, probably the biggest criminal in Edinburgh. First made his mark in the nineties, started in drugs, moved into prostitution, identity fraud, money-laundering, you name it. These days he's semi-legit, in property and development, with half the council in his pocket, but he's still a thug at heart. Smart, though, never got caught himself, always got someone else to take the bullet.'

'Until now, it would seem,' Price said.

'I can't believe it, Frank Whitehouse is dead.' Rose shook her head.

'We haven't had a formal identification yet,' Price said. 'A couple of officers are away to collect Mrs Whitehouse, escort her to the morgue.' He nodded at two men in overalls. 'We're just about ready to remove the body.'

'Can we see?' Rose said.

Price raised his eyebrows and thought a moment, looking around.

'Follow me.'

He lifted the flimsy tape and guided them under. He strode up to where the two overall guys were kneeling. Billy hung back, cricking his neck, rubbing his aching shoulders, feeling damp under his armpits. They were amongst gorse bushes now, mustardy flowers and thorns everywhere. Horseflies and midges skittered around them. A bee zig-zagged between blossoms. DI Price and Rose were in front of him, looking at the body. He crept forward until he was almost between them.

He recognised the shoes. Expensive brown leather. Scuffed. He could see now that the socks on the ankles he held last night were burgundy. He raised his eyes. Fitted grey suit, cornflower-blue tie. Sturdy chest underneath, thick neck. The face was the same scraped and bloody mess Billy remembered.

He turned and staggered out the bushes, swiping at midges, his forehead wet with sweat. He made it ten yards then fell to his knees and threw up, his vomit blood-red from the beetroot schnapps, tearing at the lining of his throat as he retched and coughed.

He ran his tongue around his mouth and spat. He spotted

two orange capsules among the mess. He carefully picked them out of the red swill and put them on his tongue, tried to swallow. He worked up some saliva and threw his head back.

He heard footsteps. Rose and DI Price were standing over him.

'It's his first dead body,' Rose said. 'He'll be fine in a minute.'

5

They spoke to the woman who found the body. Five minutes on a doorstep in West Richmond Street jotting down her middle-class shock and trauma in quotable chunks. Rose did all the asking, Billy in a daze, his mind and stomach churning.

'Nice bit of colour for the piece,' Rose said as they came away. 'We need to get something more meaty, though.'

She turned to him. 'You've got a car, right?'

Billy nodded.

'Rankeillor Street?'

'Yeah.'

'OK, let's drive to the Whitehouse place, wait for the merry widow to get back from the morgue. Catch her with her guard down.'

They headed up St Leonard's Street, Billy a step behind.

'There's no way Frank Whitehouse topped himself,' Rose said. 'And there are plenty of rivals who wanted him dead. Oh boy, we are so ahead of the curve on this story, thanks to the lovely detective inspector.'

She gave Billy a cheeky smile. He could see how she would've been a real beauty in her day. Hell, she still had it, despite the crow's feet and smoker's cough.

'He's a widower, you know. Gets lonely being on your own sometimes.'

Billy stared at her. 'You're sleeping with him?'

'Don't be so crude, a bit of human companionship never did anyone any harm.'

They turned into Rankeillor Street.

'Speaking of which, how are things with Little Miss Sunday Supplement?'

Rose had a thing about Zoe. Hard-working, veteran crime reporter for the *Evening Standard* versus privileged lifestyle and fashion journalist on the Sunday paper. It wasn't hard to fathom the resentment.

'Fine.'

'You're awful quiet today, Kiddo.'

Billy was trying to work out everything. Frank White-house. They'd hit him, left him in the trees. Dead, apparently. But he was found two hundred yards away at the bottom of the Radical Road. What the fuck?

They were at the car now. Billy patted his pockets. Charlie had the keys.

'I'll need to get the keys, wait a second.'

He went inside and met Zoe coming out of Charlie's room.

'Jesus, Billy, where have you been?' She glanced behind her. 'Charlie, Billy's back.' She turned to him. 'I texted you.'

Billy pulled out his phone. Three texts, right enough. He hadn't even noticed.

Charlie came out, hair a mess, bleary-eyed. 'Fuck's sake, Bro, what are you playing at?'

'I've been working with Rose. At a crime scene. Salisbury Crags.'

Zoe looked shocked. 'Was it . . .?'

Billy nodded. 'The guy we hit. But he wasn't where we left him. He was hundreds of yards away in the bushes at the bottom of the Crags.'

'How can that be?' Charlie said.

'You tell me, you're the one said he was dead.'

'He was.'

'Then how the fuck did he end up somewhere else?' Billy felt the stings in his hands throb, his neck muscles bunch up.

'Oh God,' Zoe said.

'Cooee?' Rose was in the doorway at the other end of the hall. 'Don't mind me, dearies. Looks like you all had quite a night of it. Kiddo here has already puked at a crime scene this morning. Billy, we need to get going in case the red tops get wind of this.'

'Cool.' Billy turned to Charlie. 'I need the car keys.'

'You OK to drive?'

'I'll have to be.'

'Where are you going?'

Billy looked at Rose waiting in the doorway and lowered his voice. 'We're going to interview Mrs Whitehouse, the wife of the dead man, who happens to be Edinburgh's biggest fucking crime lord.'

'Holy shit.'

'Yeah.' Billy turned and left.

Outside, he unlocked the car and he and Rose got in. The seats were warm in the sun, the air stale. He wound down his window as Rose put her seat belt on. He stared at the steering wheel, tried to stop his hands shaking. He put the key in the ignition but didn't turn it.

'You OK?' Rose said.

He didn't speak.

'You're not still drunk from last night, are you?'

'I'm fine.'

He still hadn't turned the key.

'Look, if it's about being sick back there, don't worry about it. I was the same the first time I saw a stiff. You get used to it pretty quickly, trust me.'

Billy turned the key and the engine started straight away. Mum's car had always been reliable, had seen them through some tough times.

He pulled on his seat belt and grabbed the gearstick. Vibrations from the engine chugged up his arm and through his body, like he and the car were part of the same beast.

'Hey, you've got a wee chip there,' Rose said, pointing at the top of the windscreen. Billy followed her finger and saw a small crystal of cracked glass in the shape of a star. 'You better get that sorted, Kiddo, otherwise the crack will just get bigger and bigger.'

Billy put the car in gear, his feet twitching on the pedals, and pulled out.

6

Blacket Place was a leafy enclave of Georgian mansions hidden between the bustle of Newington Street and the student chaos of Pollock Halls. The Neighbourhood Watch signs were brass plaques, CCTV everywhere, and Billy's ancient Micra was making curtains twitch.

The Whitehouse place was the swankiest of the lot, a gravel drive winding round an ornamental fountain out front, Doric columns fronting a two-storey edifice that was verging on stately home. They crunched up the drive and rang the doorbell.

After a while the door opened and a fair-haired young woman answered. She had an accent, Polish or Slavic, and she threw a glare at them. She was the nanny, Mrs Whitehouse wasn't in and she didn't know when she'd be back. End of conversation, door closed.

They mooched round the side of the house, having a nosey. A huge, well-tended garden with half a forest of oak and pine, a large treehouse and a pond. To the side of the house was a four-car garage. Locked, alarms, security cameras, no windows. Round the back, a gabled pine summerhouse hidden from the main building.

'Leave, now.'

They turned. A thug in a suit, thick tattooed neck, muscles

flexing as he tapped a baseball bat against his leg. A smaller guy lurked behind, same air of menace.

'And you are?' Rose said.

'Out.'

'OK.' Rose lifted a placating hand. 'We got a little lost trying to leave this palace.'

They shuffled towards the front gate, taking a wide berth round the goons.

Rose smiled at them. 'Are you employees of Mr Whitehouse?'

The big guy shook his head and indicated the gate with the bat.

'Well, nice talking to you.'

The men watched until they reached the car. They got in, drove round the corner and stopped for five minutes, then headed back to Blacket Place, parking further away from the house. The guys were gone. Billy killed the engine, his fingers still gripping the wheel.

Rose got her notepad out. 'OK, let's think about what we've got. Edinburgh crime lord dead. There's our headline right there. We can assume he died last night.'

Billy nodded, although Rose wasn't looking for input, just using him as a sounding board.

'So what the hell was Frank Whitehouse doing up the Radical Road in the middle of the night? I don't believe he'd kill himself, and I doubt he would be up there on his own at 3 a.m. or whatever, so that rules out an accident. Which means he was taken up there and thrown off.'

Billy was still nodding. He touched the bump on his head.

Rose hadn't asked how he got it. He touched his face, pushed at the skin over his cheekbone. He couldn't feel anything. He was confused for a moment, didn't know whether it was his face or his fingers that were numb. He rubbed his hands together. His fingers tingled. His brain felt sluggish, syrupy. Those pills. At least the pain had gone for now. He looked down. His legs were jittery, like a current was passing through them. He tried to stop them but couldn't. He put his hands on his thighs but the vibrations just passed up his arms. He wound his window down and gulped air, but swarms of midges made him wind it up again.

Rose was still talking to herself, figuring it out.

'Maybe he wasn't up the Radical Road at all.'

Billy gripped his legs to stop them shaking.

'Maybe he was killed somewhere else and dumped at the bottom. Or maybe he was killed somewhere else, then taken up there and thrown off to make it look like suicide or an accident. But that's an awful long way to lug a corpse when you can just dump him anywhere. And if you're going to dump him, why not do it where he's less likely to be found? Or maybe the point was to make sure he would be found.'

Billy stared out the window, his mind fizzing. Or maybe it was a hit and run and he wasn't dead like they thought and he got up and walked away, and collapsed in the gorse. Maybe they could've saved his life if they'd called an ambulance. Maybe.

'It's all speculation until forensics come back with something.'

The gears in Billy's mind ground together.

'What sort of things can they find out?'

'It just depends. It's not like *CSI*, but they sometimes come up with a useful nugget. Precise cause of death would be handy.'

Billy thought about that for a minute.

'I reckon the Mackie boys must be the prime suspects,' Rose said. 'I wouldn't be surprised if the cops have brought them in for questioning already, checked their alibis.'

Billy raised his eyebrows.

Rose looked at him. 'Wayne and Jamie Mackie. For a crime reporter, you really don't know much about Edinburgh's criminal underworld.'

'You're supposed to be teaching me.'

'How did you get this job again?'

A running joke. Rose and the paper's editor and news editor had been the interview panel. The other two had wanted another candidate with more experience, a hotshot young woman from down south. Rose had talked them into hiring Billy. She sealed it by pointing out he'd be cheaper and she could train him up. She reminded him at every opportunity.

'Yeah, the Mackies had the most to gain, rival criminal gangs and all that, and they're just about the only guys in town capable of something like this.' Rose looked at Billy. 'It takes a lot of bottle to kill someone, you know. More than you'd think.'

A lot of bottle, thought Billy.

A silver Lexus swept past them and turned into the Whitehouses' drive.

'Aye, aye,' Rose said. 'Look lively.'

She huffed as she got out of the car, and Billy followed. She scuttled to the house as he caught her up.

The car had stopped at the front door and a man and a woman got out. The car drove on to the garage, the driver waiting for the garage door to slide upward electronically.

The couple were walking up the steps, the man with a hand placed on the small of the woman's back. He was short and skinny in a loose suit, she was taller, red hair to her shoulders, wearing a black polo neck, tight skirt and heels. She had a graceful walk.

'Mrs Whitehouse?' Rose called out as they approached.

Both figures turned at the door. The man had close-set eyes and stubble. He tried to steer the woman inside the house but she didn't budge. She wore large, round sunglasses. Billy was struck by how beautiful she was – old-style, full-figured glamour.

'Mrs Whitehouse, I'm Rose Brown from the *Evening Standard*, I wondered if we could have a quick word.'

The man stood in front of the woman. 'Adele has nothing to say to you.'

'Mrs Whitehouse?' Rose looked past the man at her.

The man snarled at Rose. 'If you don't leave immediately, I'll call the police.'

'Was it your husband, Mrs Whitehouse? At the morgue?'

The man stepped forward and pressed a finger into Rose's chest. 'You don't want to mess with me, darling, I can bring you a world of fucking pain, believe me.'

Rose smiled at him. 'Can I quote you on that?'

'Here's a quote for you,' the man said. 'My brother Frank

was a much loved husband and father, and an upstanding member of this community.'

'So it was a positive identification. Mrs Whitehouse, how do you feel about the suggestion that your husband committed suicide?'

The woman raised a hand to her forehead, but Billy couldn't tell what she was thinking. He noticed some discolouration of the skin around her right eye and cheek, the edge of a bruise.

'Fuck off,' the man said. 'Frank didn't kill himself.'

'So you suspect foul play?'

Billy almost laughed at the quaint phrase Rose had used, like something out of Miss Marple. He couldn't take his eyes off Adele Whitehouse. She hadn't said anything yet. He wanted to hear her voice.

The man was right in Rose's face now, spit on the corners of his mouth as he spoke.

'When we find out who killed Frank, they're gonna wish they'd never been fucking born. And you can quote me on that.'

'Thank you, I'll do that. Mrs Whitehouse, do you have anything to add?'

She turned from Rose to Billy. Billy wondered what colour her eyes were.

'No comment,' she said.

A soft accent. A hint of west coast.

She turned and walked into the house. Billy stared at her figure, the sway of her red hair on her shoulders, the confident strut in those heels.

'You heard the lady,' the man said, giving Rose a gentle shove. 'Now fuck off and leave us alone.'

'Of course.'

The man walked into the house and slammed the door.

'So sorry for your loss,' Rose shouted after him. She turned to Billy. 'Nasty little prick. Did you notice her shiner?'

Billy nodded.

Rose laughed a big, throaty laugh. 'A crime lord dead in suspicious circumstances, a vengeful brother, an abused widow. Oh boy, have we got a front page to write.'

7

'This is dynamite.' Tom McNeil sat in his office looking at his computer screen.

Rose grinned. 'Isn't it?'

The editor turned to Billy, who was tangled up in an uncomfortable metal chair. 'Old-school reporting, doing the footwork, doorstepping the story,' he said. 'You could learn a lot from Ms Brown here.'

'I already have.'

'Screw blogs and tweets, this is real news.'

Billy had already had this lecture when he was hired. Modern mass media and digital formats were all very well, but old-fashioned foot-pounding journalism, getting out there and actually covering a story, blah blah.

McNeil was the same generation as Rose, and Billy could see what he was getting at up to a point, but they were on their way out. The whole newspaper industry was dying. The vast majority of his fellow Napier students had wound up writing online content in one form or another. He was one of the few working in print. And that wasn't out of any principles, just the only job he could get, like snaring the last berth on the *Titanic* right before it launched. Lucky boy.

Billy looked at McNeil as he talked, and wondered if Rose had slept with him too. McNeil was a solid and handsome fifty-five, sleeves rolled up, broken nose adding to the rough charisma. Billy tried to think of himself at that age, but couldn't get his head round the idea.

Just like this story. Rose had written it up in two hours like the pro she was. Leading on the suspicious death, using Dean Whitehouse's choice quotes about his brother, alluding to Adele Whitehouse's bruising, rounding up with the dog walker who found the body and the police call for witnesses.

It was all way ahead of the curve. The police hadn't officially even given out Frank's name yet. The tabloids would be sniffing, but not too hard, it wasn't a major story until the Whitehouse name came out, just another jumper.

They were dismissed from McNeil's office with pats on the back. Billy excused himself and went to the toilets. He splashed water on his face, then took two of Charlie's pills. His head was pounding again, the pain swimming into his neck and shoulders. He wondered how long it would take the pills to kick in.

He tried to think, but his mind was sludgy. A muscle twitched under his left eye. A tingle spread across his face, the feeling back after the numbness of earlier. There was a sharp pain across his temple and something flashed in the corner of his eye. He moved his head in that direction, but it was gone. There was a whiff of something amongst the stench of urinal cakes, an electrical burning smell, then everything went black. The last thing he felt were his legs crumpling beneath him.

*

Cold tile against his ear. The sound of water trickling in the urinals. Disinfectant smell.

He opened his eyes and look at his watch. Hardly any time had passed. What the fuck? Must be the stress and shock. He was so fucking tired. He felt full of fatigue, his bones aching at the joints. His headache was still there. The cold floor against his face was soothing, but he dragged himself up and checked in the mirror.

He didn't look too bad, considering. He splashed some more water on his face, dried himself with paper towels then left.

On the mess of his desk was a Post-it note: 'Go home and get some sleep, you look like you need it. I'll chase police and forensics, see you tomorrow. Good work today, Rose.'

He grabbed his bag. Instead of heading for the exit he crossed the first-floor mezzanine, through open-plan desks, towards the front of the building. There was an unofficial apartheid in operation, the Sunday paper journalists spread out across the front of the building in the flagship position, the *Evening Standard* and the daily paper down the two flanks. Mixing wasn't encouraged.

He spotted Zoe at her desk, pointing at a computer screen. Two plucked and tanned thirty-somethings hovered behind her ergonomic chair and nodded. Zoe had her hair up in a bun, a pencil through it.

The two *Sex in the City* types frowned as he reached her

desk. She looked up, surprised. He'd never come to her desk before.

'Can we talk?' He looked at her colleagues. 'In private.'

Her eyes widened. 'I'm kind of in the middle of something here.'

He looked at her screen, saw a two-page layout of tasselled handbags. He remembered as students they used to laugh together at the vacuous nature of lifestyle journalism. Not any more.

He walked away, heart stuttering against his ribs.

8

He could feel the thud of a hip-hop beat as he stood digging for his keys. He opened the door and got a blast of Wu-Tang Clan. He followed the noise downstairs and found Charlie at the kitchen table with a sandwich in one hand, fingering the touchpad of a laptop with the other. A San Miguel bottle sat sweating on the table.

Billy grabbed a remote and turned the docked iPod off. Charlie looked up and swallowed a mouthful of sandwich.

'Hey, Bro.' He pointed at the laptop. 'Just checking to see if there's anything about our little incident last night.'

'Little incident? Is that what you think it was, a little incident?'

Charlie took a swig of beer. 'OK, calm down. I'm only saying. Doesn't look like there's anything come out about it yet, anyway.'

'There won't be. We're first with the story, no one else has it yet.'

'How did you manage that?'

'Rose is sleeping with the detective inspector in charge of the case.'

Charlie laughed. 'Naughty girl.'

He took another bite of sandwich. Billy watched him chew then turned away. His stomach felt tight.

Charlie pointed at the laptop again. 'Been googling your man Whitehouse, quite the little one-man crime industry. Well, two-man, seems he did everything with his brother Dean.'

'I met him at their house. Little shit.'

'Brotherly love, eh?'

'He threatened to kill whoever was responsible for Frank's death.'

Charlie looked at Billy and slugged his beer. 'Look, we're going to be OK.'

Billy stared at his brother. 'How the hell can you say that?'

'Because it's true. We just have to stay calm.'

'In case you hadn't noticed, me and my boss are investigating this story.'

'And?'

'What if Rose finds something out?'

'How is she going to do that?'

'I don't know, we haven't had the forensic report yet. That could incriminate us.'

Charlie smiled. 'It's not going to say he was killed by a red Nissan Micra at 2.30 a.m. at that exact spot on Queen's Drive, is it?'

'I have no idea what it's going to say. Anyway, he wasn't killed there, was he?'

Charlie didn't speak.

'Did you hear me?' Billy's voice rose and he swallowed hard.

'I heard you.'

'You said he was dead last night. On the road.'

'I thought he was.' Charlie's voice had gone quiet and his eyes were on the laptop screen.

'Really?'

'Of course.'

'Maybe you just didn't want me to report it, so you said he was dead. That way, he was already gone, we couldn't have saved him anyway.'

'That's not how it was.'

'Look at me.' Billy's head was pounding, his neck muscles strained. He felt dizzy.

Charlie's gaze didn't budge from the screen.

'Look me in the eye,' Billy said, 'and tell me you thought he was dead.'

Charlie looked up and stared straight at Billy. 'I thought he was dead.'

'Promise me.'

'I promise.'

Billy shook his head.

'Look,' Charlie said. 'I was fucking loaded. We all were. And we were in shock. I made a mistake. He must've been past help anyway.'

'But he got up and walked two hundred yards.' Billy felt his legs twitching. He grabbed the back of a chair to steady himself.

'Yeah, and then he died. Anyway, I don't know why you're wasting your time worrying about Frank Whitehouse. Word on the net is that he was a nasty piece of work and the world's better off without him.'

Billy had both hands on the back of the chair now, gripping hard.

'He had a son.'

'What?'

'You heard. Five years old. Ryan.'

Charlie shrugged.

'Charlie, we both know what it's like to grow up without a dad.'

'OK, I feel sorry for the kid. But we're getting way off the point here. We did the right thing.'

'I don't think so.'

'And I suppose you'd rather be locked up in jail on a murder charge?'

'Of course not.'

'What then?'

'You were only worried cos we were all on those stolen pills of yours.'

'I didn't see you turning them down in the bar.'

'You weren't interested in saving me, you were only interested in saving yourself.'

'If that's all you think of me, Bro, it breaks my heart.'

'Fuck you, Charlie, don't get all superior with me. I know you.'

'I had to make a decision, you and Zoe were rabbits in the headlights. I did what Mum would've wanted.'

'Stop fucking using Mum like that.'

'She wouldn't want us to destroy our lives over this.'

'I said leave her out of it.'

'Reporting the accident would've been like disrespecting her memory. Is that what you want to do, disrespect Mum?'

Billy lunged for his brother, grabbed his shirt and shoved him so that the two of them spilled off the chair and on to the floor, beer and sandwich flying. They struggled on the ground for a while, Billy trying to punch Charlie but only glancing the side of his head, his knuckles crunching into the floorboards. Charlie backhanded Billy across the face, knocking him sideways and bringing tears to his eyes, a sting of blood to his cheek. Charlie scrambled on top and used his weight to pin Billy down, holding his wrists against the floor in a gesture of surrender. It was all over in a few seconds, Charlie getting the better of his little brother as usual.

'Just relax,' Charlie whispered in Billy's ear.

Billy was struggling to get free from the weight of his brother, but Charlie had a firm hold, a lifetime's experience of keeping Billy pinned down.

'Take it easy.' Charlie spoke softly, like he was comforting a baby.

Billy's breathing slowed and the tension left his body. He caught his breath back. 'It's OK for you, I have to follow the story. It's in my face all the time.'

'I know.' Charlie was still holding Billy's wrists and sitting on top of him. 'It's fucking stressful, I understand that. I know all about stress. I deal with dying people every day at A&E, you think I don't know? But we just have to stay cool, and this will all blow over.'

'You think?'

'We have to keep it together. Help each other through.'

44

Billy looked at his wrists, Charlie's thick fingers still holding tight. 'I'm OK, you can let go now.'

Charlie considered this for a moment, then released Billy's wrists and stood up.

Billy pushed himself up on his elbows and rubbed his cheek where Charlie had slapped him. It felt alive with blood, just below the surface.

'Sorry about that,' Charlie said.

'It's OK.' Billy looked at the mess on the floor, bits of sandwich floating in a pool of beer.

'I'll clean up,' Charlie said.

He offered a hand out. Billy took it and got up. Charlie put a hand on Billy's shoulder.

'Why don't you try to get some sleep,' he said. 'You look like shit.'

Billy stood rubbing his neck.

'That whiplash still bothering you?'

'Yeah, a bit.'

'Want something for it?' Charlie pulled a couple of blister packs from his pocket, one painkillers, the other sedatives. He handed both to Billy.

'Two of each should sort you out. Just keep the packs, in case you need more.'

Billy looked at the packets in Charlie's hand. 'Keeping me doped up and out of trouble, yeah?'

Charlie gave a mock reproachful look. 'Just trying to help my wee brother out. Is that a crime?'

Billy took the packs and pocketed them.

'Maybe I should go for a lie down.'

'Now you're talking, it'll all seem better once you've had some proper rest.'

Billy turned and went upstairs, leaving Charlie to clean up the mess. At the top of the stairs he stopped. He looked back down. The Wu-Tang Clan had started up already, quieter this time.

He walked to Charlie's room, went in and opened a drawer in the bedside table. It was full of medication. He rifled through the drawer until he spotted a brand name he knew was methamphetamine – Anadrex. They'd laughed about it in a club once because it was one letter away from toilet roll. He popped two pills out and swallowed them, then stuck the rest of the packet in his pocket and left.

In the hall he picked up his bag, pulled the strap over his head and let himself out of the front door, making sure to pull it closed softly so that it made no sound.

9

He kidded himself that he was just out for some air, but he knew where he was going.

His feet took him to the end of Rankeillor Street and he turned left into the bus fumes and noise of South Clerk Street. Kebab houses, corner shops, pubs and greasy spoons, the pavement in the early evening teeming with people heading home from work or out to the pub. He walked until South Clerk Street became Newington Road, past cafes and wine shops, smarter flats towering above, cleaner stonework and larger windows.

He turned left on Salisbury Road. Bigger buildings, Victorian built, darker stone, walled gardens, a hotel and a medical centre. He felt a familiar chemical rush, the same flood of energy he'd had the night before, a comforting aliveness, a welcome loss of control.

At the end of Salisbury Road he stopped. The Commie Pool was across the road, shrouded in scaffolding and infested with cranes. Behind that Salisbury Crags and Arthur's Seat glimmering in the early evening sun, the volcanic rock brought to life by the low, angular rays.

To his right was The Crags pub, a large Georgian sprawl, part of a chain aimed at students. He'd avoided it as a student, thinking himself above the sports clubs and booze cruise brigades. Anyway, he'd gone to Napier across town, mostly populated by locals, while Edinburgh Uni down the road seemed a magnet for a certain kind of braying English loudmouth. Zoe had done English literature there, then Napier's magazine journalism postgrad, where Billy had somehow hooked up with her, despite feeling she was out of his league. He still had a lingering niggle that she was slumming it with him.

Charlie had run with the arrogant medical student gangs for a while, but even he'd got tired of the constant one-upmanship and lager-fuelled bravado. Not that he didn't still come out with his fair share of bullshit. But maybe he was right about Mum, about last night. Maybe it was the right thing to do. Didn't make it any easier.

Billy realised he was grinding his teeth and chewing on the inside of his cheek. He could feel the tiny particles of enamel and skin in his mouth. It was incredibly dry, his tongue too big and swollen.

He skittered into The Crags car park. Stopped at the door. Over to his left was a beer garden, a spread of sticky picnic benches sitting on concrete slabs. Just beyond that was a five-foot wall, topped by a latticed wooden fence, barbed wire snagged along its top edge. He knew exactly where he was and why he was here. Over that wall was the White-houses' garden.

He stared at the barbed wire for a moment then shuffled into the pub.

It was quiet, a few punters scattered around on the sofas. A young barman in regulation pub T-shirt flicked through the *Evening Standard*. Must've hit the streets not long ago. He closed the paper as Billy approached.

'Pint of Stella,' Billy said.

The man started pouring.

'Mind if I take a quick look at your paper?'

'Knock yourself out.'

Billy turned the paper to face him on the bar. EDINBURGH CRIME LORD DEAD. Rose had the headline she wanted. The standfirst named Frank and suggested suspicious circumstances. He scanned the familiar story, looking to see if there had been any edits before going to print. The picture was a dramatic shot of Salisbury Crags, police tape and forensics in white overalls in the foreground.

'Quite something, eh?' the barman said as he clunked the pint down.

'Yeah.'

'Right on our doorstep.'

Billy felt a tightening across his chest as he paid for the Stella and passed the paper back. He struggled to breathe until he was out of the door and heading for the beer garden, staring at the back wall of the Whitehouse place.

He slumped on a bench and gulped at his pint. He had a fierce thirst. One of the other tables outside was occupied – four girls in hockey club sweatshirts and ponytails. They watched him for a moment then went back to their conversation. He stared at them, then looked over at Salisbury Crags for a moment. Then he turned and looked at the wall.

His left leg was trembling. He put a hand on it but it didn't stop. He spilled some beer on his jeans, then got up, glugging his pint, and walked towards the wall. He tried to put on a nonchalant amble, like he was just stretching his legs. He walked the length of the wall to the back of the beer garden and pretended to study a sign detailing the rules and regulations for the pub car park. The hockey girls occasionally glanced over at him.

He stood there drinking till his glass was almost empty, then turned and began sauntering back. Took a final few gulps of beer, his hand shaking as he lifted the pint to his lips. Put the empty glass down on a table then began striding towards the Whitehouses' back wall. The hockey girls were watching him but he didn't turn round.

He got to the wall and grabbed the rough stonework, hoisting himself up so that he was quickly on top, his body pressed against the fence there. He laid his hands carefully on the barbed wire at the top of the fence, then brought his foot up to the same level. As he put his weight on it, the fence wobbled and the wire dug into his hands. In a quick movement he heaved himself up and on to the fence, the barbs piercing the skin of his palms, the wooden lattice creaking under his weight, then he launched himself into the Whitehouses' back garden.

He stared at his hands.

Drops of blood were forming at several small puncture wounds. He crouched down and wiped his palms on the grass. The lawn was cut short and his hands left dark streaks across the nap of the grass.

He straightened up and looked around. He could see the

pond and the treehouse, one wall of the main building. The foliage of the trees dappled everything in evening sunlight.

The air was still, clogged with pollen, gangs of midges dancing in the light as he took a few steps forward. The summerhouse was to his left, sitting in a suntrap out of sight of the main house. The sun glanced off the large front window. Behind the window, he thought he saw movement.

The reflection of the sun was blinding, his head thudding. He remembered the painkillers in his pocket. He fished them out and took two, snorting phlegm into his mouth to swallow them.

He crept towards the summerhouse. As he got nearer, the angle of the reflected sunlight changed and the inside of the building was revealed. Sitting on a low, cream sofa was Adele Whitehouse, no sunglasses, hair tied back from her face, bare feet tucked under her. She had a small copper hash pipe raised to her lips, a lighter held to the bowl. Her eyes were closed and she was inhaling deeply.

Billy walked forwards, drawn by the sight of her. He was only a few yards away when she opened her eyes and turned to face him. Her right eye was bruised and discoloured. She stared at him for a long moment, then invited him in with the smallest twitch of her head.

He opened the summerhouse door and stepped inside. The air was stifling, thick with the sticky smell of skunk. He closed the door. She indicated the space on the sofa next to her. He sat down, unable to take his eyes off her.

She held out the pipe and lighter. He took them, put the pipe in his mouth and lit it. A sweet burning in his throat and lungs, pressure and heat building as he held his breath. He exhaled. An immediate bolt to his brain made his eyes widen. He repeated the process, more ready for it this time, breathing out evenly. He handed the pipe and lighter back. She held his gaze as she took them.

'I didn't get your name earlier.' Her voice was soft and syrupy.

'Billy Blackmore.'

She raised her eyebrows. 'Nice to meet you, Billy Blackmore. Do you want to tell me why you're creeping around my garden?'

Billy stared at her. She was maybe early thirties but looked younger, faint lines around the eyes the only giveaway. She still wore the black polo neck and skirt, her bare knees exposed.

'I came to see you.'

She raised her palms. 'Well, here I am.'

She reached for a tin sitting on the arm of the sofa. It was full of skunk. She crumbled some into the bowl of the pipe and took another hit, breathing out through her nose.

'And why did you want to see me, Billy Blackmore? To get your story? The grieving widow and all that?'

'What happened to your eye?'

Adele raised a hand to it, turned her face away from him a little. She pulled a scrunchie out and let her hair fall free, brushing it forwards to partially cover the eye. She laughed as she did it.

'You know how to make a girl self-conscious, don't you?'

'Sorry.'

He was staring at the tender skin around her bruised eye.

She smiled. 'I walked into a door.'

He smiled too. 'Can I quote you on that?'

'Is this an interview?'

'We're just talking.'

'We are, aren't we?'

Billy nodded at her eye. 'Did Frank do that?'

Adele frowned and looked away.

'Sorry, none of my business.'

She turned back, offered him the hash pipe.

'Of course it is, you're a newspaper reporter, aren't you? Everything's your business.'

He took a hit and sank further into the sofa. Her bare feet were six inches away from his hands. He noticed that his leg twitch of earlier had stopped. Adele's feet were small, carefully manicured, crimson varnish on the nails. He imagined reaching out and stroking her feet, massaging them and moving his hand up her tanned, bare legs. His brain felt soupy with the skunk and the painkillers and everything else. He handed the pipe back.

'I'm sorry about your husband.'

'You don't have anything to be sorry about. You didn't kill him.'

Billy watched her suck on the pipe as silence cloaked them. He noticed her lips were sticky and sparkly with gloss. He wondered what they would feel like against his.

'So you think he was killed?'

'I expect so. People were queuing up.'

'Which people?'

53

A sound came from his bag on the floor. His mobile. He stared at the bag but didn't move. His arms felt heavy.

Adele nodded at the bag. 'You'd better answer that. Probably your boss lady, wanting to know if you've got the scoop.'

He took the phone out of his bag. The screen said 'Zoe'. He switched it off and put it back. He spotted his digital recorder and pulled it out.

'Would you mind if I got a couple of quotes?'

Adele laughed. 'So you really are here to interview me? Here's me thinking you were just worried about my welfare.'

He looked at her, didn't speak, the recorder still in his hands.

She gave him a sly look.

'Are you going to mention in your article that we shared a skunk pipe?'

'I think we can leave that detail out.'

She pointed at the machine. 'How do I know you've not had that on the whole time?'

'You don't.'

She sighed and filled the pipe with more skunk. The air between them was a swirling green haze.

'Go on then, switch it on.'

He fumbled with the buttons till a red light appeared, then held it close to her. It felt intimate, shared.

'OK, how did it feel to find out that your husband was dead?'

She gave him a flat look. 'Devastating.'

'If you'll excuse me for saying so, you don't sound particularly devastated.'

She lit the skunk pipe and took another hit. Held it in her lungs. Billy held his breath too, watching her. She breathed out, wet smoke billowing into his face. She nodded at the recorder as if it was an eavesdropper.

'Of course I'm devastated, what are you trying to suggest, that I didn't love my husband? Frank Whitehouse was a caring, devoted and loving father and husband, that's the appropriate thing to say at a time like this, isn't it?'

'Have you told your son yet?'

A cloud came over her face and she looked down. 'No.'

'What are you going to tell him?'

'Good question.'

'What about you, how do you feel about it?'

'You've already asked me that.'

'I don't think you were being entirely honest with me.'

She fixed him with a gaze. 'Have you ever seen a dead body, Billy Blackmore?'

'I'm asking the questions.'

'Let's do a trade, I ask one, then you.'

Billy thought about it. 'OK.'

Adele passed him the pipe. He had to put the recorder down to take it. He placed it on the sofa, almost touching her bare leg.

'So, have you ever seen a dead body?' she said.

'Yes.'

'And how did it affect you?'

'It's my turn to ask a question.' Billy breathed smoke into the thick air.

Adele made an acquiescent movement of her hand.

'How did it really feel to find out your husband was dead?'

'Terrible. My turn. What was it like when you saw the dead body?'

'Shocking. It was your husband.' Billy thought of the crash last night. 'At the crime scene. This morning. I vomited.'

Adele shook her head. 'At least I didn't do that at the mortuary.'

'My turn,' he said. 'Do you think your husband committed suicide?'

'Not in a million years. He could no more kill himself than spread wings and fly off Salisbury Crags. My turn. Do you always flirt with recently bereaved widows?'

'You're the first. Do you always flirt with journalists right after your husband's death?'

'You're the first. How long have you been a reporter?'

'Almost a month.'

Adele laughed at that. 'Wow, they sent the hardened pro to get the scoop, eh?'

'No one sent me. What I said at the beginning was true, I came here to see you.'

'And yet here you are getting your quotes. Do you feel like a big-boy crime reporter now?'

'No.' Billy handed back the pipe. 'To tell you the truth, I feel out of my depth.'

Adele took the pipe but didn't put it to her lips. She stared in Billy's eyes for a long time, Billy holding her gaze.

She looked away. 'I know what you mean.'

'Can I ask about your black eye?'

She looked at the digital recorder. 'That's enough.' She

picked it up, trying to work out the buttons. 'How do you switch this thing off?'

He put his hand on hers as she held the machine. She took his hand and turned it over.

'You've been bleeding.'

He looked down. A smattering of red marks on his palm, a constellation of blood. He pulled his hand away.

She handed him the recorder and he switched it off and put it in his bag. When he looked up, she was staring past him.

'Shit.' She threw the pipe and lighter into the skunk tin, then placed that in a handbag tucked under the sofa.

Billy turned at the sound of the summerhouse door opening. It was a small boy in a *Star Wars* T-shirt, carrying a plastic lightsaber. He wrinkled his nose at Adele, didn't even look at Billy.

'Mummy, it stinks in here.'

'Yes, it does, darling. Where's Magda?'

'We're playing hide and seek. I'm hiding.'

Billy got up, felt the full force of the skunk on his wobbly legs. 'I'd better go.'

The boy still hadn't looked at Billy. He was making lightsaber noises and swinging it at a plant in the corner of the room.

'Thanks for the quotes,' Billy said.

Adele looked at him as he picked up his bag and slung it over his shoulder. She went into her handbag, pulled a card out and handed it to him. Her name and mobile number.

'If you need anything else. Anything at all.'

His cheeks felt hot and he suddenly needed fresh air. He opened the summerhouse door and gulped. Behind him he heard the boy.

'Who was that man, Mummy?'

'He's no one, darling. Now come and give your mummy a cuddle.'

10

He had three missed calls from Zoe and a couple of texts from Charlie wondering where he was.

Instead of heading back to Rankeillor Street, he turned right before Scottish Widows. A trickle of students were coming and going from Pollock Halls. They looked unconcerned about life, joking and laughing. He walked past them down Holyrood Park Road to the roundabout. He knew where he was going.

The barbed-wire cuts stung his hands as he dialled Rose's number.

'Hold the front page,' he said when she answered.

'Ha, ha. What's up? I'm in the middle of something here.'

'I've interviewed the widow.'

'Adele Whitehouse? You beautiful boy. How did you manage that?'

'I climbed over their back wall. Met her in the summerhouse. She agreed to speak.'

Rose gave a laugh. 'Hot damn, we'll make a crime reporter of you yet. How was she?'

Billy thought a moment. 'Grieving.'

'She say anything interesting?'

'The usual platitudes.'

'How did she seem? Genuinely upset?'

Billy thought about the skunk pipe, the flat voice, the flirting. 'Yeah, I guess.'

'Did you ask her about the eye?'

'Says she walked into a door.'

'A sense of humour in adversity, that's good, we can use that. Wait a minute.'

Her voice disappeared for a second. Billy heard a man's voice he recognised in the background.

'Rose, are you with the detective inspector?'

'Never mind that, we've got another front page to write. I had a follow-up already done for tomorrow's first edition, but there wasn't much in it. The Mackies have alibis, there's no news about Frank's whereabouts on the night, blah blah. What you've got is better. I'll call McNeil. Get down to the office and start knocking it into shape.'

Billy was at the top of Queen's Drive. The evening sun had set, but twilight still bathed the cliffs and the park, the gorse a subdued umber in the shade of the Crags.

'I'm on my way.'

'Good. I'll meet you there in an hour.'

'That give you enough time to finish off our friendly bobby?'

'Enough cheek out of you, Kiddo.' Rose was laughing as she hung up.

His phone rang. Zoe. He diverted the call and put his mobile away.

He began walking down Queen's Drive. The trees where it happened were a hundred yards away. Cars chugged up and down the slope. Billy scanned them, looking for a red

Micra. He hadn't seen another one since yesterday. He felt dizzy as he tried to focus on the cars blurring past. He looked ahead. He was seventy yards away. His legs were struggling, like wading across the ocean floor. The thud of his heart seemed irregular, speeding up then slowing down. The left side of his face was fizzing with subdued pain. It felt like the skull under his skin was itchy, an itch he couldn't scratch. Fifty yards. There was a flash of red in the corner of his eye. He thought about his collapse in the toilets at work. Smelt the air. Gorse and petrol fumes. Tarmac beginning to cool in the evening breeze. Thirty yards. A red car streaked past. Not a Micra, not even close. Twenty. He stared at the road, saw a small dark stain. Fifteen. Could be blood, engine oil, dogshit, roadkill, anything. Ten yards. His legs were making him speed up. The stain had dried into the rough surface of the road. He held his breath, his pulse beating against his temples, his throat constricted, his heart thundering now, his face and hands stinging in time, blood bursting to escape his body.

He kept walking. He was past. Heading downhill, speeding up, his body relaxing, his fingers loosening their grip on the strap of his bag. His face still tingling, his mind stepping back from the edge.

He walked and didn't look back.

*

'I hereby officially change your nickname from Kiddo to Scoop.'

Rose had just finished reading a printout of his story, going through it with a pen, marking up occasional changes.

'Congratulations, one month in and you've got a front page. Took me two years.'

She threw the printout on to his desk.

'Make those changes and we'll run it past McNeil. He's going to love it.'

Billy looked at Rose's corrections. He'd written it straight – grieving widow, suspicious death, crime lord and all that. He'd cut Adele's quotes to make her look more sympathetic, more caring. Used the detail of the son for the human angle. Rose had tweaked it to suggest more, highlighted the black eye, tabloided it up a little, but not too much.

As he made the changes, his phone rang and he got two more texts. He didn't pick up the phone, concentrating on the story. He finished up, emailed the copy to Rose and McNeil then picked up his bag and walked to Rose's desk.

'Think I'll call it a night, if that's OK?'

'Of course, you've done more than enough. Good work today. You have a wee jar with your mates and get some sleep. I'll see you tomorrow for the police press conference. Should be good, they'll have the forensic report by then.'

'Really?' Billy felt light-headed. 'You got the inside track from the detective inspector?'

Rose gave him a coy look. 'No, forensics are working on it through the night, it's a high-profile case. We'll just have to wait and see what they come up with.'

Billy rubbed at the bump on his head. It seemed harder than before, as if his brains were calcifying.

Rose looked concerned. 'You OK?'

'Fine.'

'Have you had that checked out?'

'My brother says it's just a bump.'

Rose nodded. 'How did you do it, anyway?'

Billy shook his head. 'You don't want to know.'

*

He pushed open the door of the Holyrood and went in. Smell of expensive foreign lagers and home-made burgers. He looked around. The last text from Charlie said he was here. The three of them used to live in this place as students, when it was run-down and full of bikers and crusties. It had closed for a bit and been refurbished, but they hadn't ripped the heart out of the place. It was halfway between classy bar and scruffy dive.

He spotted Charlie at a table with Zoe. Charlie had a trumpet-horn weissbier glass in his hand, Zoe fingering an enormous glass of red wine. They were alternately staring at each other then looking down, talking quietly, their faces lit by a candle on the table, their hands almost touching. They looked like a couple out on a romantic date. Billy stood and stared at them, some old-school indie washing quietly around the place.

He went to the bar and got two weissbiers and a red wine. He popped two Anadrex and a couple of Oramorphs out of their packets and swallowed them with the wheat beer. The barman stared at him. Billy stared back.

'What?'

'Nothing,' the barman said, and went to serve another punter.

Billy took the drinks over to the table.

'Here you go.'

Charlie and Zoe looked up.

'Christ,' Zoe said, reaching for him. 'Sit down, we've been worried sick.'

'Yeah, I can see that.'

'What's that supposed to mean?'

Billy stared at her. Gorgeous green eyes. He'd missed looking into those eyes. He thought of Adele's eyes, tried to picture them through the skunk smoke.

'Nothing.'

'I called you loads of times.'

'I've been at work. Sorry.'

'I thought you had the rest of the day off?' Charlie said. 'Last we spoke you were heading to bed.'

'Needed some air. Ended up getting involved in something.'

Zoe ushered Billy into the seat next to her. 'Like what?'

'I interviewed the widow.'

'Jesus,' Zoe said. 'Can't you just stay away from this?'

'It's the biggest story the paper's had in years, and the *Evening Standard* has the exclusive. There's no way I can avoid it.'

'You didn't have to interview the wife, though,' Charlie said.

'Widow,' Billy said. 'Not wife.'

'Whatever.'

'Her husband's dead, remember? We killed him.'

Zoe looked at him. 'Calm down, honey.' She had her hand on his wrist. He felt his skin itch under her grip and moved his arm to lift his pint, shaking her off.

'I've got tomorrow's front page,' he said. 'From talking to Adele.'

'Adele?' Zoe said.

'Mrs Whitehouse. The widow.'

Charlie frowned. 'What did she say?'

'The usual.'

Zoe touched his hand again. 'Listen, you need to leave this story alone.'

'I can't. I am the fucking story.'

Charlie took a drink. 'Can't you have a word with Rose, cover something else?'

'How would that look? As a trainee I just got a front page, an interview that no one else got, and I suddenly ask to cover some bullshit vandalism case in Craigmillar? I don't think so.'

'We're just concerned about you,' Zoe said.

Billy took a big drink of beer. On the wall behind Charlie, amongst old brewery mirrors and landscape prints, was a framed green and blue map with MAKE YOUR OWN PATH stamped across it in thick red capitals. Billy choked as some beer went down the wrong way. Zoe rubbed his back. He put his beer down, still staring at the sign.

'There's a police press conference tomorrow morning at St Leonard's. They're expecting to have the forensic report.'

'Christ almighty,' Charlie said. 'That doesn't matter. They're not going to come up with anything.'

'You don't know that.'

'Yes, I do.'

'How?'

Charlie had no answer to that.

11

'Jesus, Scoop, you stink of bevvy.' Rose led him into the media room of St Leonard's police station. 'And you look like shit. I said have a few jars, not the whole pub.'

Billy let himself be guided. They skulked at the back by the coffee machine. They could've been in any anonymous beige conference room in the world, windows shut, light slipping between the blinds. It was already warm outside and starting to heat up in the room. The place was full of hacks and shutter-monkeys. Two camera crews with presenters had set up near the front. Rose's story yesterday naming Frank Whitehouse had lit the fire under all their arses. The nationals and television were playing catch-up, and Billy's front page, due in an hour, was another step ahead. A few reporters approached and congratulated Rose on her story, fishing for a slip of the tongue.

'Just sit there and don't say a word.' Rose pushed Billy into a seat and sat next to him.

'Did you not manage to get an advance report on the forensics from Loverboy?'

'Shut up.'

Billy had meant it as a joke and was surprised by her tone. She glared at him.

'Number one, Stuart Price is a good man. Honourable and

decent. Number two, don't go blabbing about where we get our information. The room is full of Scotland's biggest dickhead journalists, for God's sake. Remember that.'

There was a bustle of activity down the front as DI Price came through the door, followed by a uniformed female officer. Behind her was Adele Whitehouse in a tight grey suit, large dark glasses. She looked composed, the glamorous widow, the full Jackie Kennedy.

'The ice maiden cometh,' Rose whispered. 'Looks like she could bust a few balls. How the hell did you get her to speak to you?'

'Natural charisma.'

Rose studied Billy as he stared at Adele. 'You're a cute son of a bitch, but don't get cocky. One story doesn't make you.'

DI Price began proceedings in that dull formal monotone policemen always use at press conferences. Billy wondered if they learned it at media training.

'I'd like to welcome you all to St Leonard's today for this press conference concerning the body that was found at the bottom of Salisbury Crags yesterday morning. I'm sure you all know already, although the information has not been formally released until now, that the person in question was, in fact, local entrepreneur Mr Frank Whitehouse.' Price looked to Adele next to him. 'We have with us Mrs Whitehouse, who will say a few words at the end of today's meeting, but she will not answer any questions. Please direct any questions to me.'

Adele sat motionless and inscrutable as cameras flashed at her. Her hair was down, falling in red waves over her shoulders, brushed in such a way as to partially hide her right eye. Billy couldn't see any bruising, maybe she'd done a make-up job on it. She was beautiful in her stillness, a vision of stoicism amongst the attention of the room.

'As I said, Mr Whitehouse's body was found at the bottom of Salisbury Crags, and initial police investigations were centred around the possibility that he had fallen or jumped from the Radical Road above.' Price lifted a few sheets of paper in front of him. 'But the results of a forensic examination of the body and the immediate crime scene would now seem to suggest that Mr Whitehouse was not killed in a fall of any kind. His injuries were inconsistent with such a death, rather the forensic team felt that those injuries were most likely caused by an automotive incident of some kind.'

Automotive incident. Quaint phrase. Billy remembered the impact, the sound of Frank's body rolling over the roof, his own head cracking against the glass. He reached for the bump on his temple and felt suddenly hot, couldn't catch a breath in the stifling air of the room.

'We are therefore now confirming that the case of Mr Whitehouse's death is a murder investigation. Since Mr Whitehouse was not found on or next to a road, it is so far unclear as to whether he was involved in an incident some distance away and his body transported to the scene of his discovery, or whether indeed he was not killed outright by an accident and somehow walked away from it, only to collapse at the bottom of the Crags. We are therefore returning to the area around the foot of the Radical Road for further forensic examination of an extended crime scene, and you will be informed of the results of that process when we have them.'

Price paused for breath. Adele lifted a hand to touch her glasses and a dozen camera flashes blitzed the room. Billy's head and neck pounded, the pain in sharp jabs coursing down his back. He shifted in his seat and tried to swallow.

'I'm sure there will be no shortage of speculation from you ladies and gentlemen of the press about the nature of Mr Whitehouse's death, given his high profile and reputation. But let me remind you most strongly that this is now an active murder investigation, and excessive speculation in the press at this time may in fact prohibit a fair trial, if and when we reach that stage. Given Mr Whitehouse's position in this city, we will be pursuing a number of lines of enquiry. Let me just now put out an appeal to the general public, though. We are keen to hear from anyone who might have seen Mr Whitehouse between the times of 2 a.m. and 5 a.m. on Monday morning, whether it be in the vicinity of Salisbury Crags or elsewhere. The last confirmed positive sighting of the deceased was at Fingertips massage parlour in Jock's Lodge, an establishment that was one of several Mr Whitehouse owned. That was at approximately 1.50 a.m. Fingertips is some twenty or thirty minutes' walk from where Mr Whitehouse was found, the direct route between the two places passing through Holyrood Park, and we would ask if any revellers or late-night drivers saw the deceased or anything at all suspicious anywhere along that route, that they contact the police immediately.'

Billy pictured the headlights of the taxi, fingers of light

stretching towards them as they struggled with Frank's body. He could hear the chug of its engine as it slowed to pass their parked Micra. He felt his palms and cheeks tingle, unearthly feelings like itchy pains, signals from his mind that his body couldn't decode. His left leg was jittering. A muscle under his eye twitched. He closed his eyes, felt the heat of the room smother him. Eventually he opened his eyes. Price cleared his throat and looked a little uncomfortable.

'One other important point to mention, which could be pertinent in our investigation, is that on the occasion of the last sighting of Mr Whitehouse, he was accompanied by his family dog, a distinctive border collie with a white patch over its right eye. The dog was wearing a plain leather collar but unfortunately nothing to identify it or its owners.' Price paused, looked down at the desk. 'The dog answers to the name of Rebus.' There was a smattering of nervous laughter in the room, quickly snuffed out as Price looked up. 'Apparently Mr Whitehouse was a fan of the fictional detective. The deceased was found with a dog lead in his pocket, but so far the dog has yet to be located.'

A dog. Rebus the fucking dog. Where was he? Billy pushed the heels of his hands into his eye sockets and tried to breathe. He never saw a dog. Adele never mentioned a dog. Adele. He raised his head to look at her. He pictured her without the glasses, the look on her face, the damaged skin around the eye.

'Mrs Whitehouse will now say a few words,' Price said, causing a maelstrom of flashes.

Billy felt dizzy at the rushing sound of shutters clicking,

the stifling room suddenly bathed in unnatural light, Adele lit up as if on a red carpet. She cleared her throat and spoke quietly but firmly, reading from a piece of paper.

'First I want to say that Frank was a loving father and husband, and both Ryan and I will miss him more than words can express. He was a decent man, despite what some people, including members of the press, have said about him. He worked hard to provide for his family, and we are all devastated by his death.'

She raised a hand and touched the arm of her glasses. Cue flashes. Billy felt disoriented and turned away. He spotted a familiar figure standing in the doorway to the right of the desk. Dean Whitehouse. Black suit, black tie, face like stone. He was staring hard at Billy.

'I always knew Frank couldn't have committed suicide,' Adele said. 'And now we know that his death wasn't an accident either. I can't begin to express my anger and outrage over this, and I implore anyone with information about my husband's murder to come forward to the police as soon as possible.'

Her head came up, triggering a mass of camera flashes. Billy had to close his eyes for a moment, then reopen them. With her shades on, Adele could've been looking at any of them, but Billy felt as if she was staring right into him.

'Please.' There was a tiny crack in her voice. 'Please help us find who did this to Frank. If not for me, then for the sake of our son, who's lost his father.'

Billy wanted to console her, take her in his arms and squeeze until everything was all right.

'Thank you.' Adele got up. There was a crescendo of noise, camera flashes going off, reporters shouting her name, DI Price trying to calm things down.

A burst of energy swept through Billy and he jumped from his seat. He propelled himself towards the door Adele was heading to, where Dean was waiting with an arm outstretched for her.

'Adele,' he shouted, his voice lost in the chaos.

She glanced round then turned away through the door.

Dean glared at him then followed her.

The skin bristled all over Billy's face and neck, like an electric shock. Small bursts of light exploded in the corner of his vision like mini fireworks. He caught a smell of something, burnt coffee or a whiff of the skunk he'd shared with Adele. A pain leapt across his left shoulder and surged into the back of his neck. He felt his legs go from under him. He knocked a chair over on the way down, heard Rose shout his name, then his vision blurred and his mind emptied as he collapsed on the floor.

12

The whole length of Queen's Drive was closed off. Billy stood at the top staring at the curve of road stretching down and round past the *Standard* offices, Dynamic Earth and the parliament. Police officers were congregating at various stages on the slope, milling about, swapping jokes and banter.

Billy stared at the police ROAD CLOSED sign. Cars approached the roundabout next to him, slowed as they took in the sign, then circled and headed back the way they had come.

He'd only passed out for a few seconds. Same as in the toilets. What was happening to him? He came round on the floor with Rose over him, her hefty cleavage in his line of sight, thick perfume filling his nose.

'I'm fine,' he said, before she'd had a chance to speak.

He tried to pick himself up as calmly as possible, managed to get to a chair, fingers tight on the blue plastic.

'Must've had a dodgy pint last night,' he said.

Rose stared at him, compassion in her eyes. 'Go home and get some rest. Call me when you feel better.'

He hadn't gone home. He needed fresh air, time and space to think.

He turned now and walked across the grass, away from

the road, uphill then left to the bottom of a path. The start of the Radical Road. No name anywhere, just a red and white triangular sign warning of falling rocks. No tarmac, just gravel. Not a road at all. How had it got its name?

He started up the slope, his legs unsteady, feeling the stones in the path through the soles of his trainers. The sun was hammering down from a cloudless sky. What the hell was with this weather? He took his jacket off and pushed his sleeves up, felt sweat under his arms. The stink of gorse blossom everywhere. He imagined the pollen clogging his nose and throat. His tongue felt sticky. A few bees meandered in and out of bushes to his left. It was too early in the day for midges, thank God.

He passed another sign, a battered, metallic *Historic Scotland* plaque stuck to a boulder. 'DANGER. Please Beware of Falling Rocks'. The path became grassy underfoot, ochre sandstone cliffs rising to his right, a steep yellow slope falling away on the other side. It didn't take long before he was high up, more than a hundred feet, looking down at the police activity below.

Behind him the cliffs loomed, and in front the fall was equally dramatic. He stopped and looked around. He could see for miles, from the Pentlands to the Forth bridges and Fife. The light diffused to a vague haze in the distance, but the foreground was painfully sharp in the morning light. He could see down Rankeillor Street from here. He thought he spotted the Micra parked in the road, a smudge of red. He could see the police station, the newspaper office, the Holyrood. In the other direction, The Crags pub and Adele's house. His whole world enclosed in a small turn of the head. And of course down below, the small cluster of trees on Queen's Drive. There were no police there yet, they were all still standing around on the grass, waiting for instructions, sipping coffee from cardboard cups. He wondered if he would ever escape from this world. If he deserved to.

He reached out and touched a flower on the nearest gorse bush. He picked it, crushed the petals in his fingers and brought them to his nose. A smell like honey. He reached back out and grabbed a thorny branch in his fist. The thorns dug deep. His hand reacted instinctively to pull away but he forced it to remain, gripping tighter until the individual pinpricks of pain smeared into one, his whole hand on fire. He squeezed his fist in a slow pulse, feeling the thorns respond, digging deeper into his flesh. Eventually he pulled his hand away. More blood. More pain. Like the barbed wire. Like the nettle stings. All infusing into one.

He leaned over the edge. Long way down, almost a sheer slope, smothered in thick spiky bushes all the way. An easy way to die. You would get ripped to shreds on the way down. He leaned further out. His head throbbed and his mouth sweated. He forced himself to stand still, his eyes losing focus as he stared down to the bottom.

Eventually he stepped back and took a deep breath. Everything was normal. The bright sun, the faint drone of traffic in the distance, a thin breeze making the gorse quiver a little.

His phone rang. He pulled it out. Adele.

'Hi,' he said.

'Are you OK?'

'Fine. You?'

'I'm stoned. Apparently you had a funny turn at the press conference.'

'Hangover. It was too hot in there.'

Billy heard a lighter fizz into life, then a breath.

'I want to see you,' she said.

Billy looked at the distant hills, which seemed to be closing in on him. 'Sure. When?'

'Now. Come to my place.'

Billy looked in the direction of her house. It was mostly shrouded by trees, the grey roof peaking through.

'The summerhouse again?'

'No, just come to the house. I'm alone.'

She hung up. Billy looked down to the expanse of grass below. The police were slowly walking towards Queen's Drive, ready to examine the road in detail.

His neck throbbed. He tried to crick it, but it just hurt more. He pulled out a pack of painkillers, took three and then made his way down the Radical Road.

13

She was sitting on the back patio gazing at nothing when he emerged from the trees at the bottom of the garden. She wore a thin green blouse and tight jeans with a small rip in one knee. She was fingering the frayed edges of the ripped denim and smiled when she saw him.

'You came over the back wall again.'

'I wasn't sure what the protocol was.'

'You could've just rung the front doorbell.' She looked at her watch, a delicate silver thing. 'You were quick.'

'Don't like to keep a lady waiting.'

Billy rubbed a thumb across the palm of his hand and winced. The pain was muffled, but he was still acutely aware of it.

'More trouble with the barbed wire?'

He stepped on to the patio. She didn't get up. There was a stoned glaze in her eyes.

'It's fine.'

'Let me see.'

He thought about it for a moment then held his hands out. She took them in hers.

'Jesus, what a mess. Let's get you cleaned up.'

'There's no need.' He didn't pull his hands away.

She got up, still holding his hands, and led him into the kitchen like a little kid. She turned a tap on.

'Run them under there for a bit.'

She rummaged in a cupboard, then came out with a first-aid kit. The kitchen was huge, a marble island in the middle, heavy copper pans hanging like fruit from a tree, Smeg fridge sulking in the corner, jars of pasta and rice on a shelf next to hardback cookbooks. It was like one of the rooms they always featured in Zoe's magazine, full of expensive, unattainable shit. Zoe would love this place.

Adele handed him a tea towel. He rubbed at his hands. Small spots of blood appeared on the fabric.

'Sorry,' he said.

'Come here.' She took his hands. 'This might sting a little.'

She wiped them with something antiseptic. Her head was down, concentrating on what she was doing. Billy stared at the top of her head, the intricate swirls of hair, the infinite spread of follicles. He could smell her shampoo, coconut and some exotic fruit. He looked down and saw she wasn't wearing a bra under the blouse. Rounded nipples and full breasts, larger than Zoe's. His hands stung but he held them steady. She began spreading some kind of cream on the cuts, a slow circular motion across his palms that had him mesmerised.

'It's like you're reading my fortune.'

She smiled and played along, putting on a fake-ominous voice.

'You will have a long and happy life.' She traced a crease in his skin with her finger. Billy noticed she wasn't wearing any jewellery. No rings. Her nails were short but neat, glossy and deep red, same colour as her toes.

'Really?'

'Oh, yes. You will marry a very beautiful woman and have six healthy children. You will become a rich and successful journalist.'

'Sounds great.'

Adele frowned. 'But what is this?' She stroked a line that bent round the edge of his palm, touching the hairs on his wrist and making them tingle. 'This is bad, very bad.' She was trying to keep a straight face. 'This line here means you will always carry a darkness within you, a terrible secret you can never tell to another living soul, one which will torment you to the grave.'

'Ouch.' He flinched.

She dropped the voice. 'Sorry, did that hurt?'

He shrugged.

'Well, I'm done anyway.' She packed away the first-aid kit. 'You should really get them bandaged, but I don't have anything suitable here.'

'My brother is a doctor, I'll speak to him.'

'You do that.' She looked around the kitchen as if searching for something. 'Would you like a drink?'

'Why did you invite me here?'

She raised her eyebrows. 'It's rude to answer a question with a question.'

'OK. Yes, please, I would like a drink. Thank you. Now, why am I here?'

She got gin from a cupboard and tonic from the fridge.

Billy watched the denim stretch tight across her arse as she bent to reach things.

'Don't you like me?' she said.

'I hardly know you.'

'We got on well enough last time.'

'I was interviewing you, it's my job to be nice to interviewees.'

'But you said yesterday you hadn't come to interview me.'

'That's true.'

'So we did get on?'

'I thought so.'

She was focusing on the drinks, chopping a lime, pushing ice out of a tray.

She turned, handed him a drink and held his gaze.

'You don't seem very upset by your husband's death,' Billy said.

'Let's not talk about him.'

'But I'm a crime reporter, that's my job.'

'You're not here on official business, are you?'

'Not if you don't want me to be.'

'I don't.' She raised her glass. 'Now drink with me.'

They both took large slugs. Mostly gin, just a ghost of tonic.

Billy made a show of looking round. 'Where is everyone?'

'Magda has taken Ryan out for the day.'

'Have you told him?'

Adele took a large drink. 'I've tried. He doesn't really get it. He's more worried about Rebus, he misses that stupid dog like crazy.'

'What about Dean? I get the impression he's looking after you at the moment.'

'He thinks he is.'

'He's been sticking to you pretty close. I'm surprised he let you out of his sight.'

'Me too.' Adele frowned. 'He's virtually moved in here. He seems to presume that because I was Frank's wife, that somehow possession of me is just going to pass over to him or something.'

'So where is he?'

'He took off with his two stooges after the press conference. Said to wait here, not go out and not speak to anyone. Very charming. I have a feeling he's about to stir up a lot of trouble.'

'How do you mean?'

'I think he's looking for the Mackie boys. He believes they killed Frank.'

'What's he planning to do if he finds them?'

'It won't be pretty.'

'Is he as nasty as he looks?'

'Nastier.' Adele touched her bruised eye.

'He did that to you?'

She turned away. 'Things are complicated.'

'I don't give a shit how complicated they are, it's no excuse.'

'It's nice of you to care.'

She put her drink down on the worktop and moved closer to him, pressing against him. He could see her nipples through the blouse. She placed a hand lightly on his chest.

He heard a noise. Voices. Men's voices. The sound of a key in a lock and the front door opening.

'Dean, fuck.' Adele was already pushing him towards the patio doors. 'Get out.' She pushed him through the doors and pulled them closed with a click.

The large spread of lawn seemed too exposed. He crouched against the back wall, breath hammering in his lungs, trying to calm down. He could hear conversation inside.

'Where have you been?' Adele sounded calm, annoyed almost.

'Why, did you miss me, darling?' Dean's voice.

There was laughter – gruff, male. Dean's goons.

'Hardly. Just hope you didn't get into any trouble.'

'We're not the ones in trouble, eh, lads?'

More laughter.

'What's that supposed to mean?'

'Nothing for you to worry your pretty head about. Just remember, me and the lads have been here with you the whole time since the press conference, OK? Understand? It's important you don't fuck this up.'

'What did you do?'

'Nothing, darling.' Dean laughed. 'I told you, we've been here all day.'

His voice receded as he left the kitchen. 'Now, fetch me a beer, there's a good girl.'

Billy launched into a crouching run, heading for the bottom of the garden, his heart thumping, not daring to look back.

His phone rang as he tried to keep his legs steady up Dalkeith Road. Charlie.

'Hey, Bro, what are you up to?'

Billy glanced behind him at the Whitehouses' back wall and The Crags' car park. 'Just walking.'

'Does the name Jamie Mackie mean anything to you?'

'One of the Mackie boys.'

'Cunt's just been hauled into A&E with suspected shotgun wounds. Looks like we've got ourselves a little vendetta going on.'

'Christ.'

'Exactly.'

'How is he?'

'Hard as fuck, by the looks. Took a hit to the leg and one to the arm, but has been sitting swearing his head off the whole time. He'll be fine once he's patched up.'

'God.'

'Might work out nicely for us, though.'

'How do you figure that?'

'Takes the heat off. Two big criminal gangs in the city taking potshots at each other. Tends to overshadow the original incident. Don't you think?'

'I can't believe you're talking like this.'

'How should I be talking?'

'You're a cold bastard, Charlie.'

'Cold doesn't come into it. Just looking out for my little brother in his moment of need.'

'Spare me.'

'That's what I'm trying to do. Spare you any more grief. Did you manage to get Rose to move you off the story?'

Billy thought about Adele's hand on his chest. 'Not exactly.'

'Shame. Right, I'd better dash, lives to save and all that.'

Charlie ended the call. Billy stared at the phone in his hand. He flicked through the address book and called Rose.

'Hey, Scoop. Thought I told you to get some rest.'

'I'm fine.'

'It doesn't look too clever, my protégé collapsing at a bloody police press conference.'

'It was the heat. And the hangover.' He forced a laugh. 'I really want to get back to work.'

'Well, I suppose you could cover something else. There's a safe cycling initiative being launched in Granton later.'

'Come on, Rose, don't be stupid. This is my story, I got the interview with the widow.'

'Haven't been round there again recently, have you? Could do with another exclusive.'

Billy raised a hand and stroked the bump on his temple. 'No, but I have got something for you.'

'What?'

'Jamie Mackie has just turned up in A&E with gunshot wounds to his leg and arm. Not sure if the police even know about it yet.'

Rose chuckled. 'Holy shit, Scoop, why didn't you lead with that? How do you know?'

'My brother just called.'

'Good God, you're on fire at the moment.'

'Thanks.' Billy wondered where he was going with this, what he was doing. How long could it all go on? 'So, what's our next move?'

'Come pick me up at the office.' Rose sounded excited. 'We've got a hospital to visit.'

14

'Busy for a Tuesday lunchtime.' Rose looked around.

Billy followed her gaze. It took a moment for his eyes to get accustomed to the gloom after the bright sunshine outside. A builder with his hand wrapped in a red towel. A gang of schemies, two of them flat out on chairs, seemingly unconscious. Several old people holding elbows or stroking knees, looking worried.

They waited a few minutes till the receptionist was distracted by an ambulance pulling up outside, then they walked through double doors into a long corridor with treatment tables, some cordoned off by white plastic curtains. Rose had an assertive swagger as she approached each occupied treatment area and peaked round the gaps in the curtains. Billy lagged behind, watching her in awe. She was so confident, so sure of herself. He couldn't imagine ever being like that.

They were halfway down the corridor when Billy spotted his brother. Billy had never seen him at work. He actually wore a white doctor's coat and had a stethoscope round his neck, like he was playing a dressing-up game.

Charlie spotted them and approached, glancing round. 'What the fuck are you doing here, Billy?'

Rose stuck out a hand. 'Good afternoon, Dr Blackmore.'

Charlie switched on a smile. 'Nice to see you, Rose.'

'Likewise.'

Charlie took Billy's arm and tried to turn him round. 'You shouldn't be here.'

Rose interrupted. 'We'd like to see a good friend of ours who has apparently been brought in. Jamie Mackie?'

Charlie ignored Rose and stared at Billy. 'What do you think you're doing?'

'I just told you . . .' Rose said.

'I wasn't fucking talking to you,' Charlie said.

'Can I quote you on that, Dr Blackmore?'

Charlie stared at her. 'I'm afraid I have to ask you to leave.' He put an arm out to Rose's shoulder, ushering her out of the treatment area. 'You could get me into trouble.'

'That's the last thing we want to do. So maybe you could direct us to our friend Mr Mackie, and we'll be out of your hair.'

Charlie smiled. 'You can't see him, he's in surgery.'

'Nothing too life-threatening, I hope?'

Charlie had succeeded in turning them round. Rose and Billy reluctantly allowed themselves to be pushed towards the exit. 'I'm sure my brother has told you about Mr Mackie's condition. There is no further information at this time. You would need to ask the surgeon about his condition once he comes out of theatre.'

'And when do you think Mr Mackie will be out of surgery?'

'Who knows?' Charlie stared at Billy, who still hadn't said a word.

Charlie stood with them at the door. Outside, paramedics helped an elderly woman out of an ambulance and into a wheelchair.

'Now, please leave.' Charlie turned to Billy. 'I'll speak to you later, little brother.'

Billy watched Charlie head back into the A&E ward. He seemed so grown up, dressed like a doctor.

'Oh my God, this just gets better,' Rose said under her breath.

Billy turned. Three hard-looking schemies – two guys and a girl – were striding towards them, the two guys smoking, the girl checking her phone.

Rose nudged Billy. 'The one in the middle is Wayne Mackie. This should be good.'

The three of them pushed past Rose and Billy and up to reception.

'Where the fuck is my brother?' Wayne shouted.

The receptionist was middle-aged and sturdy, didn't look as if she took any shit. She peered over bifocals at him.

'It's no smoking in here, sir.'

'Never mine that, you fucking bint, I asked you a question.'

'You'll need to take your cigarette outside, sir.'

The calmness of her voice made Billy smile. Wayne was furious.

'Are you fucking listening to me, ya hoor?'

'If you continue to speak to me in that aggressive tone, I shall be forced to contact security and have you removed.'

'Fuck's sake.' Wayne leaned over and grabbed the front of

the woman's blouse, pulling her towards him. 'If you do that I'll find out your address and wait till you're asleep one night and come over and fucking torture you till you wished you were dead.' He pointed his cigarette towards her like a dart, ash falling on to her blouse and smudging. 'Now, if you don't tell me where Jamie Mackie is right this second I'm going to stub this fucking thing out in your boss eye.'

The woman was beaten, Billy could see it, Wayne could see it.

'Mr Mackie is in surgery at the moment,' she said quietly, trying to retain dignity.

'When will he be out?'

'If you wait here, I'll see what I can find out.'

Wayne let go. She straightened her blouse and walked away.

'Excuse me,' Rose said. It was only then Billy realised he was standing with her next to Wayne and his two mates. When had they walked over? His head buzzed.

Wayne spun round. 'Who the fuck are you?'

'Rose Brown from the *Evening Standard*. I was wondering how you felt about your brother being shot?'

Wayne snorted with mock laughter. 'How the fuck do you think I feel? Fucking raging. I'm gonna kill those White-house cunts.'

'I beg your pardon?'

'You think I don't know who fucking did this? That wee cunt, Frank's brother. Thinks we had something to do with Frank's death. But that was fuck all to do with us. Not saying I'm sorry Frank's deid, likes, cos I'm not. Cunt was the bane of my life. But me and Jamie never had fuck all to do with Frank's death. The Old Bill ken that as well, we've got an alibi, hunners of witnesses saw us at the Electric Circus that night, till closing. That midget cunt Dean Whitehouse needs to watch his back after this, and you can print that on the front fucking page of yer rag, ya dozy bitch.'

'Thanks, I will.'

Rose turned and walked away. Billy tried to move his feet, but they wouldn't budge. He stared at Wayne Mackie, at the shaving rash on his neck, his Yankees baseball cap, his pinched face. He thought about what it would be like to have your brother shot in broad daylight, or hit by a car in the street.

'What the fuck are you looking at, you lanky streak of piss?'

*

'OK, thanks for that. Speak to you later.' Rose ended her call.

Billy was behind the wheel, heading into town along Old Dalkeith Road, stopping and starting at each set of lights. His legs trembled and his neck ached with every jerk of the car. It was so hot in here. He wound the window down, didn't make any difference. He needed a cold drink.

'Well?' he said.

'Drop me at the office and I'll write it up. Oh boy, we're the new Twitter, we're so ahead of the game on this bloody story.'

'And what about me?'

'I want you to go to the Edinburgh Dog and Cat Home on Seafield, see if they've had a dog fitting the description of the Whitehouse mutt handed in.'

Billy braked hard, skidding to a stop at a pedestrian crossing. A worried mum with a buggy stepped out into the road, giving Billy the evil eye.

'Fuck off.' Billy felt sweat on his brow, and swiped at it.

'Don't use the language of the gutter with me, Scoop.'

'This is my story and you're sending me off on a fucking dog chase?'

'Firstly, this is not your story, it's ours, for the *Evening Standard*, got that?'

'I got you Adele's first interview, and the reaction from Wayne Mackie.'

'And you did great, but you can't do everything.'

He thought of Adele in the house with Dean and the other two men, capable of anything.

'Fuck it, I'm going to the Whitehouse place, get a quote from Dean.'

Rose shook her head. 'No point. He's been taken in for questioning.'

'What?'

Rose nodded at her mobile. 'DI Price said. They have Dean, Adele and the two bodyguards in the station right now, checking their stories.'

A car horn blared behind them. They were still sitting at the pedestrian crossing, the light green. Billy crunched the car into gear in a fluster and jerked forward.

'Take it easy with the gearbox.' Rose patted the dashboard. 'Us old dears take a bit of looking after, you know.'

He kept his eyes on the road as he churned through the gears. They headed up the hill towards the Pleasance.

'Look,' she said. 'I'm sure there will be plenty more opportunities for big stories here. But you need to learn how to do the donkeywork as well as the headline stuff, OK? If you find the dog, that'll be big anyway. If we find out where it was found, that could help with the investigation. And imagine the kudos if the paper returns the mutt to the wee boy, eh? That human interest stuff will shift copies, believe me.'

They turned at the bottom of the Pleasance and headed for the office. Billy tried to relax his body behind the wheel, but his hand on the gearstick and his other on the steering wheel were vibrating with ten years' worth of engine rattle, the growl of it echoing in his forehead and chest.

He pulled up and Rose got out.

'Go find that dog.'

15

As he got out and locked the car door he was hit by the sharp tang of sea air, so familiar to him as a kid. He'd grown up only a few minutes along the road from here in a poky two-bedroom ex-council flat on Portobello High Street. He bristled with memories, the rubbery skin of a dead jellyfish on the beach, ice cream melting on his hand, his mum licking it off and laughing. Worrying as his and Charlie's dinghy drifted away from land, his mum becoming a spot on the horizon, Charlie reassuring him they were fine, they would paddle back soon.

The Edinburgh Dog and Cat Home was a functional pebble-dashed block, worn by salty winds. He went inside. The air was thick with the stench of animals and urine, cooking in the sunlight. Yelps and barks, hissing and scuffling paws created a chaotic swarm in his head.

Their mum had never let them have a dog, claimed she was allergic. Billy sneezed thinking about it, imagining cat hair floating in the yellow air around him.

A skinny girl with blonde frizzy hair and braces on her teeth greeted him at reception. *Morna* on her nametag, pinned to a boyish uniform. Billy explained why he was there, asked if they'd had any collies found recently that might fit the description. This was stupid, there was no way the dog would've been handed in. What were the chances? He should've done this over the phone.

'There was a collie brought in yesterday,' Morna said. She had that distinctive posh Edinburgh accent, like Zoe's. When had he last seen Zoe? He wondered how she was.

'Really?'

'I can show you if you like?'

'That would be great.'

As they walked through to a corridor full of kennels, noise erupted, yowls and growls on all sides, the rattle of metal cages scraped by claws. Morna took him towards the far end, where a small black and white dog with a scruffy coat was huddled in a corner. It looked up at him and its tail thumped half-heartedly against the concrete floor.

It wasn't the Whitehouse dog. No white patch on its face. It looked as if it had been longer on the loose than a couple of days as well, ribs showing under the fur, a hungry, hunted look on its face. The dog stared at him but didn't get up.

'Rebus?' he said.

'What?' Morna said.

'It's the dog's name, apparently it's called Rebus.'

'Like the policeman?'

'Yes, like the policeman.' He turned to the kennel again and made a clicking noise. 'Rebus, here boy.'

'It's a girl.'

The dog didn't move. What was Billy doing? He knew it wasn't Rebus, no white patch and the wrong sex. But he wanted it to be the Whitehouse dog. He didn't know why it mattered, but it did.

95

He stroked a finger down the metal ribs of the cage. 'Here, girl.'

The dog came over to sniff his hand, tail wagging. She looked a little disappointed that there was no food on offer.

'Sorry, little lady, I don't have anything for you.'

'She's a good-tempered bitch,' Morna said. 'Better than some of the poor, mistreated souls we get in here.'

'And you've no idea who the owner is?'

'No chip, no collar. Even in this day and age, we still get plenty like that.'

'What'll happen if no one claims her?'

'We'll try to rehome her. Shouldn't be too tricky, collies are very popular.' Morna looked along the corridor at a string of dogs pacing and pawing. 'It's the Rotties and Staffies we have trouble with. They're much more aggressive, less suitable for families.'

'Do you ever have to put them down?'

'Occasionally, but only the ones with serious temperament problems.'

Billy looked at the dog in the kennel. She licked his hand, the tongue rough and ticklish against the wounds on his palm. He stood up.

'You know, I've been thinking of getting a dog for a long time myself.'

Morna frowned at him. 'Really?'

'Yeah. Maybe I could take this one?'

'It's not as simple as that, there's a lot to consider. Do you have time to spend with a pet? Money for vet's bills and food? Does your lifestyle have room for a demanding animal?'

'I've thought about all that. I said I'd been considering it for a while.'

Morna looked uncertain. 'Collies need a lot of exercise and mental stimulation, they're very energetic and intelligent dogs.'

'Sounds perfect. Just what I'm after.'

'There are procedures to go through. You'll need to speak to one of the senior staff.'

'Fine.' Billy shrugged. 'Let's do that.'

Half an hour later he was driving up Portobello Road with the dog in the passenger seat, her tongue lolling out of her mouth as she panted and looked round.

Billy reached over and rubbed her flank.

'Who's a good girl?'

She responded by licking the back of his hand. It felt good.

The car stopped at the lights at Jock's Lodge. He looked to his right. Fingertips massage. The last place Frank was seen alive by anyone. Except Billy. The lights changed and he chugged forward. He took a left at Meadowbank towards the east end of Holyrood Park. Road still closed. He slowed and went round the roundabout, peering into the distance, but from this end you couldn't see the section of road where it happened. Had they found anything yet?

He drove back the way he had come, stroking the dog's back and feeling her ribs bumpy under her skin and fur.

16

Sitting in the Micra outside the Whitehouse place he watched Adele walk round the corner on her own. She looked impeccable as ever and she was walking fast, her hand twitching at the arm of her sunglasses as she turned into the driveway.

Billy got out of the car and beckoned for the dog to follow, making encouraging noises. He was delighted to see that she did exactly what she was told. He guided the dog across the road and ushered her in the direction of the Whitehouses' drive.

He could hear the crunch of Adele's feet on the gravel up ahead.

'Adele,' he called.

She jumped and turned. Just like the first time they met, her on the steps, glamorous and unknowable, him scurrying up the drive.

'What the hell are you doing here?'

'I came to make sure you were OK.' Billy was out of breath.

'It's dangerous.' She looked round. 'You being here. It could get us both in a lot of trouble.'

'What do you mean?'

'What do you think I mean? Dean.'

'Where is he?'

She looked exasperated. 'At the police station, I presume. They've just released me after two hours in a hot, sweaty room.'

'What did you tell them?'

'Nothing.'

'You must've told them something.'

'It has nothing to do with you.'

'I heard you and Dean from outside the back door.'

She wasn't flustered. 'All the more reason to stay away.'

Her attention was distracted by the dog.

'What's that?' she said.

'A collie.'

'I know that, idiot, what's it doing here?'

'I got it from the Dog and Cat Home. I thought maybe you and Ryan could have it.'

'Are you insane?'

'You said Ryan was missing Rebus.'

'And you thought...'

'Mummy.' The front door opened and Ryan ran towards the pair of them. Adele scooped him up into her arms and gave him a hug, holding tight for a long time.

'Oh my beautiful boy, how are you?'

'Fine.'

Her question was loaded with love, his answer was off-hand kid talk.

'Where have you been?' he said, only vaguely curious.

'I had to go out for a bit, that's all. But I'm back now.'

'Where's Uncle Dean?'

'He's talking to the police at the moment, darling.'

'Has he been naughty?'

'He's helping them find out what happened to Daddy. Remember we talked about that?'

Ryan was distracted. He pointed at Billy. 'Who's that man?'

'I'm Billy.'

Adele put Ryan down. 'Never mind about him, go back inside.'

Billy noticed Magda standing in the doorway, face tripping her.

'Is that his dog?' Ryan said.

'Yes,' Adele said. 'Now run along and play with Magda for a minute, there's a good boy.'

'I don't want to, it's boring.' Ryan looked at Billy. 'What's your dog called?'

Billy stared at him. 'I don't know.'

'You don't know your own dog's name?'

'Maybe she doesn't have one.'

'That's just silly, all dogs have names.'

'Well, what do you think she should be called?'

'Is it a girl dog?'

Billy nodded.

Ryan thought about this for a while. He reached out a hand and the dog came and sniffed, tail whipping the air. After a moment she wandered off to examine some flowerbeds.

'You should call her Daisy. There's a girl in my class called Daisy who's nice.'

'Maybe I will call her Daisy, good idea.'

'She looks a bit like our dog. But Rebus isn't here at the moment, is he, Mummy?'

Adele was trying to push Ryan up the steps. 'Go and tell Magda you can watch a DVD.'

That grabbed his attention. '*Kung Fu Panda*?'

'Sure, *Kung Fu Panda*.'

'All of it?'

'Yes, all of it.'

'Yes.' Ryan made a celebratory fist as he reached the top of the steps. He turned and waved at the dog, which was sniffing in some bushes.

'Bye, Daisy,' Ryan said, then looked at Billy. 'Maybe you could bring her back when Rebus is here, so they can play together.'

'That's a great idea.'

Ryan took Magda's hand at the door and went inside.

'Get out of here,' Adele said.

'What?'

'Dean will be back any minute.'

'So?'

'Do you think it's that easy to replace someone?'

'I didn't think . . .'

'No, you didn't. There's still a chance Rebus will turn up.'

'I'm sorry, you're right.'

Adele sighed. 'Look, it's just . . . it's all getting a bit much, you know?'

Billy heard the crumpling noise from the roof of his car in

his mind, felt the knots in his shoulders, the needles of pain in his hands.

'Yeah, I know what you mean.'

He reached out and touched her arm, but she flinched and pulled away. 'Not here.'

'Then where?'

She removed her glasses. He was surprised to see her eyes were wet. 'I'll be in touch.' She looked at the house. Magda was in the living room holding a DVD box and staring out the window at them. 'Now go, and take your stupid dog with you.'

*

He parked the Micra outside the flat. He reached past the dog and opened the glove compartment, rattled through the medication blister packs crammed in there. He hadn't realised he'd been through so many. Not enough, though, not the way he felt. He rummaged around, pushed out a couple of greens and two oranges. He was pretty sure one was amphetamine, the other morphine. Did it matter?

The dog tried to lick the pills in his hand.

'Not for you, girl,' he said softly. He swallowed the pills.

He had no idea how to look after a dog. Food. A basket? Collar and lead. Toys? He thought about how his mum had never let them have one. He pulled down the driver's side sun visor. Tucked inside was a battered old photograph. He slid it out. He and Charlie kept it there to remind them. It was the three of them on Porty beach. Billy was only six or seven. He remembered it being taken, they stopped a man walking his dog on the way past. The dog was friendly and he and Charlie nagged Mum for a few minutes, giving up when she put her foot down. They knew she wouldn't change her mind. They played on the sand, building castles, digging trenches, paddling in the icy waves, Mum relaxing on a towel in shorts and a T-shirt. They were a unit then, comfortable, content.

He stared at the picture. All three of them were squinting into the sun. Mum had her hand up, shielding her eyes. It looked as if she was trying to see into the future, peering at him now, wondering what had happened in the years since her death.

He turned to the dog.

'I don't think the name Daisy suits you.'

The dog responded by pushing her ears back keenly.

'I think we'll call you Jeanie, after Mum. How about that?' He rubbed her nose. 'You like that, Jeanie? Yeah?'

She nuzzled him as he rubbed between her ears.

He glanced one last time at the photograph of the happy family and put it back in the sun visor, folding it away. He opened the car door.

'Come on, then.'

The dog stayed in the car.

'Walkies?'

She bolted out the door, suddenly alert, tail swishing, ears pinned back, walking in tight circles.

Billy laughed. 'Walkies it is, then.'

Queen's Drive was still closed, but there were no police about.

Looking down from the Radical Road, he was struck by the quiet. No swishing car noise, no city chatter, just the occasional buzz of insect wings, the gentle padding of Jeanie's paws on the gravel and grass as she followed various smells.

He sat down on the edge of the precipice, his legs dangling over the side like a tiny child on a giant sofa. His legs felt so weary, heavy beyond words. His shoulders felt crushed by the atmosphere, hunching him over like an old man. He had to give up. He wanted to confess. Surely it would be easier than this. He tried to think about the repercussions, but his mind got lost in a haze of endless possibilities, infinite universes branching off into oblivion, each one taking an atom of his fractured brain with it. He touched the lump on his temple, the evidence of the crash there for all to see. It seemed to have hardened further. It felt alien to his body, an interloper in his system. Weren't bodies supposed to attack outside agents, protect the organism at all costs? He rubbed at the bump as Jeanie crouched close by and went for a piss. The soft patter of urine on grass, a trickle running on to the path.

'Lovely evening.' It was a middle-aged woman out walking her dog.

Billy nodded as she passed.

'Nice and quiet, with the road closed,' she said.

He tried to imagine walking into a police station and telling them everything that had happened.

He struggled to his feet, his body lurching with the pills and the pain, with everything else.

'Come on, girl.'

He made his way back down the road, Jeanie at his side.

17

He had the key in the door when his phone went. Jeanie was sniffing around the weeds poking up between cracked paving stones in their front garden. He pulled his phone out. Rose.

'Hey,' he said. 'Nothing at the Dog and Cat Home.'

'Never mind that, we've got another breakthrough. It was a hit and run on Queen's Drive, for sure.'

Billy felt his throat close up and he struggled to swallow. 'How do you know?'

'They found blood on the tarmac across from where Frank's body was found. It matches his blood type.'

'Shit.'

'I know. They also found tiny fragments of car paint at the same place. Red. They went back and checked the body – sure enough, matching paint chips on Frank's clothes.'

Billy took his key out of the door and walked down the path to the street. He stared at the Micra parked there.

'So it looks as if someone hit him on the road, then pan-icked and legged it. Or maybe they moved the body. Either way, it doesn't look like he was dead straight away. My guess is he got up and staggered away for a bit, then collapsed.'

'Right.' Billy knelt in front of the car, looking along the edge of the bonnet. The metalwork was rusty along the rim, flakes and patches of it on the grille too. He picked at a bit and it came away in his fingers.

'Question is, was it deliberate or a genuine accident? I guess this could get the Mackies off the hook if the police can't find the car and link it to them, and if their alibis hold together.'

'Have they any idea what kind of car it was?' Billy stroked the bonnet. It was warm against his palm. Jeanie came to the pavement and looked at him with her head askew, inquisitive.

'Not yet. They might get more info with further tests, but they don't seem too sure. They reckon it's quite old, apparently they can tell stuff like that from oxidisation of the metal and paint or something. Don't ask me, I'm not a scientist.'

'It could still be the Mackies though, couldn't it?'

'It might well be, Scoop. We need to do more digging. This story is not going away any time soon. Which brings me to the other reason I called.'

'Yeah?'

'How do you fancy a free pint?'

Billy suddenly felt a searing thirst. 'Could do.'

'Good. I have a request from our good friend Detective Inspector Price. He wants to meet you for a drink.'

'Why?' Billy's voice came out higher than expected.

'Take it easy, he just wants to talk to you about Adele Whitehouse.'

'Adele?'

'They had her in for questioning earlier about the Jamie

Mackie shooting. She's Dean Whitehouse's alibi, apparently. Very convenient. She was ice cold, gave nothing away.'

'What has that got to do with me?'

'Stuart was impressed with your merry widow interview. As we all were. I think he wants a chat about what she was like, why she might've opened up to you, all that.'

'Right.' Hesitation in his voice.

'I'll come along and hold your hand, OK? It's completely off the record and informal.'

'Well...'

'Good. How about The Montague in half an hour?'

'I guess.'

'See you there, Scoop.'

Billy ended the call and stared at the Micra. Mum's car. Now a murder weapon. He turned towards the house.

'Come on, Jeanie.'

The dog trotted after him as if she'd known him all her life.

He let them both in quietly. The sound of the television in the living room. One of those *CSI* things. He walked to the doorway. Charlie and Zoe were on the sofa next to each other, beers in hands. They hadn't heard him over the television. They looked completely untroubled.

'Comfy?' Billy was pleased when they both jumped.

Charlie bolted out of the sofa. 'Here he is, the lunatic little brother.' He was trying to sound casual. 'What was that all about, coming to the hospital today?'

Was that today? Billy was losing track of time.

'I told you about Jamie Mackie in confidence, you dick. I

didn't expect you to bring the *Standard*'s crack crime reporter round to give me grief.'

'It's my job, Charlie.'

Charlie shook his head. Zoe was standing up now and she seemed to be mirroring Charlie's movements. It was like they were his mum and dad, and he was a naughty toddler. They were always together. Every time he came home, there they were, fresh from talking about him. He had wondered earlier how Zoe was, now he couldn't stand to look at her.

'Charlie told me what happened,' she said. She reached out a hand, but she was too far away to touch him. 'I think you should take a break from that job, maybe even quit altogether.'

'Quit? I thought we were supposed to act as if nothing had happened? How's it going to look if I suddenly quit my job, right after getting the best interview the paper's had in months?'

Zoe looked at Charlie, clearly wanting him to speak. Charlie cleared his throat.

'We've been discussing things,' he said.

'I bet you have.'

Charlie put a hand on Billy's arm.

'Why don't you sit down?'

'I don't want to sit down.'

Charlie looked nervously at Zoe, then back again. 'Like I said, we've been talking, and I think you might be suffering from PTSD – post-traumatic stress disorder.'

Billy stared at his brother, then at Zoe. The television

blared too loud in the background. 'What the hell are you talking about? Like war veterans?'

'Kind of,' Charlie said. 'In your case, from the accident.'

Billy shook his head. 'I'm not suffering from anything except guilt because of killing someone and covering it up.'

'See, this is what Charlie is talking about.' Zoe stepped towards him. 'We all feel guilty, of course we do, but . . .'

'But I was driving,' Billy said.

'Yes,' Charlie said. 'We know. We were there, remember?'

'Don't fucking patronise me, Charlie.'

Charlie had his hands held out in a peacemaking gesture. 'I'm not patronising you, Bro.'

Billy let out a laugh and looked from one of them to the other. 'You've got it all worked out, haven't you?'

'We're worried,' Zoe said. 'You seem to be losing perspective, having to cover the story as well. Just listen to Charlie.'

'How have you been feeling?' Charlie's voice was even.

'How the hell do you think I've been feeling?'

'Any flashbacks or bad dreams?'

'Charlie, I can't believe you're trying to diagnose me with this bullshit.'

'It's not bullshit, it's a real medical condition. Have you been having panic attacks?'

Billy didn't answer.

'Amnesia, difficulty breathing?'

Billy remembered fainting in the toilets and at the press conference.

'What about strange physical sensations?'

Billy thought about his tingling body, his twitching leg,

his numb face. The throbbing pain that even now was coursing through his neck and shoulders, making him crick his neck. The solid lump on his temple, pulsing his guilty secret out into the ether.

'Look.' Charlie put an arm round Billy. He was distracted by Jeanie entering the room. She must've been sniffing out the bedrooms first, checking her new territory.

Charlie and Zoe stared at the dog.

'What the hell is that?' Zoe said.

'I got a dog.'

Charlie shook his head. 'What the fuck? Why?'

Billy shrugged. 'I was at the Dog and Cat Home seeing if they had the Whitehouse dog . . .'

'Wait,' Zoe said. 'The Whitehouses have a missing dog?'

Billy nodded. 'Frank was walking it when...'

Zoe rubbed her eyes. 'I don't remember a dog. Was there a dog, Charlie?'

Charlie sighed. 'Never mind that, what about this mutt?'

Jeanie padded calmly around as if she'd always lived there. She investigated the bin in the corner of the room.

'She's not a mutt.'

'Why the hell would you get a dog? See this is all part of what we're talking about, you're losing your grip on things.'

'People get dogs all the time. They're not all in the queue for the psychiatric ward, are they?'

'You know what I mean.'

Zoe was petting the dog now, scratching it between the ears. 'What's she called?'

'Jeanie.'

Charlie took his hand from Billy's shoulder and moved away. 'You are fucking kidding me.'

'What?'

'You called her after Mum?'

'Why not?'

'Why not?' Charlie was raging. 'Don't you see what the fuck is happening to you?'

'What do you mean?'

Charlie sucked in a deep breath and took something from his pocket. More pills. Billy didn't recognise them.

Charlie held them out. 'Ideally, you should speak to a shrink about this, but in the circumstances I don't think that's a good idea.'

'So you're just going to drug me up, is that it?' Billy clicked his fingers to get Jeanie's attention. She wandered over, un-fazed by the raised voices.

'It's not like that,' Zoe said.

'Sounds like it. What are they anyway?'

'Mood stabilisers.' Charlie showed Billy the packet. It had Tegretol stamped on it.

'Fuck off, I'm not taking them.'

Charlie gave him a look. 'You've been taking plenty of other shit. Without asking. Don't think I haven't noticed.' He offered up the pack. 'Maybe you should lay off the uppers and downers, and try some of these instead.'

Billy stared at the packet for a long time, then reached out and took it from Charlie's hand.

'Now let's all just fucking cool our jets,' Charlie said.

Zoe came over and rubbed Billy's arm. He stared at her.

'I feel like we've hardly seen you,' she said softly. 'Come on, sit down, I'll get you a beer.'

'I can't.' Billy pulled his arm away. 'I have to go out.'

Charlie sighed.

'I have to meet a copper in the pub.'

Zoe looked at him. 'Why?'

'It's Rose's fuckbuddy, DI Price. He wants to talk to me.'

'What about?'

'Adele.'

Zoe's eyes narrowed. 'Why does he want to talk to you about Adele Whitehouse?'

Billy shrugged. 'Because I got in and interviewed her, I guess. The police questioned her about Jamie Mackie. She's Dean's alibi. She didn't give anything away.'

Charlie rubbed at his forehead. 'You shouldn't be involved in this mess. Stay out of it.'

'I can't.'

'You have to, or it'll kill you.'

Billy leaned down and ruffled Jeanie's fur. 'There's one other thing you should know. The police have worked out it was a hit and run on Queen's Drive, and they're looking for a red car in connection with it.'

He left the room, Jeanie trotting after him, tail swishing. He heard Charlie over the sound of the television. 'Fuck.'

18

He'd never been in The Montague before, despite living round the corner. In a neighbourhood awash with students on happy hour, it was a dull grey old man's pub, populated by halfway jakeys and off-duty coppers from St Leonard's across the road.

There were a handful of burly law-enforcement types bursting out of their shirts and guzzling pints of Best as Billy walked in, trailing Jeanie behind. The woman behind the bar had faded tattoos and a kind face.

Billy wangled a bowl of water and bought some crisps for Jeanie, opening the packet and placing it on the floor by his feet. She gobbled at them and lapped at the water, nudging the bowl across the floor with her snout so that water spilled on Billy's trainers. He knelt down and stroked her back.

'I'll get you something proper to eat once we're finished here.'

'I didn't know you had a dog.' It was Rose standing over him. She was in a floral print dress. He'd never seen her in a dress before. Her breasts were spilling out the front. Beside her, DI Price couldn't take his eyes off them.

Billy straightened up. 'Just got her today.'

'At the Dog and Cat Home?'

Billy nodded and Rose laughed.

'You are really something. Sure you're up to the responsibility of a pet?'

Billy shrugged.

Rose put a hand on Price's chest. 'Stuart, what can I get you?'

'I'll get these,' Price said. 'The lady never buys the first round.'

Billy followed Rose to a table, bringing Jeanie's water bowl with him.

'Now,' Rose said. 'Just play it straight with Stuart, OK? He's one of the good guys.'

'I like your dress.' Billy raised his eyebrows at the low-cut front.

'Shut it.'

Price arrived with drinks.

'I take it Rose told you what this is about,' he said to Billy.

'Kind of.'

'Well, as I'm sure you're aware, I've been reasonably helpful to Rose in releasing information about the case to her early.'

'Yeah, I noticed.'

Billy looked round. They were getting more attention now from the regulars and off-duty police. A detective inspector sharing a drink with two reporters, one of them with Double Ds on display.

'Anyway, being helpful is a two-way street. So I want to talk to you about Adele Whitehouse.'

'I believe you had her in for questioning.' Billy tried to think about what he was supposed to know and what he wasn't. He couldn't get it clear in his head. Outside the window, shafts of evening sun lit up Salisbury Crags. Everywhere he went, the Crags were glaring down at him. He rattled the Tegretol in his pocket and took a swig of lager. Jeanie's ears pricked up at the noise from his pocket, then she lost interest when he pulled an empty hand out.

'Indeed,' Price said. 'She is providing an alibi for Dean Whitehouse for the time of Jamie Mackie's shooting.'

'Makes sense, the two seem almost inseparable.'

'And yet you've managed to get Adele on her own, haven't you?'

Billy paused.

'Your interview in the *Evening Standard*?'

'Of course.'

'How was she?'

Billy slugged more lager. 'I'm sorry, how do you mean?'

'Just that, how did she seem when you spoke to her? She had just returned from identifying her husband's body. She came across as measured and calm in the interview.'

'That's how she was.'

'Do you think she was in shock?'

Billy considered this. The hash pipe. The sly glances. The bare feet next to his hand. 'No, I don't think so.'

'Did she say anything about Frank? Or Dean?'

'Nothing that didn't go into the piece.'

Price sipped his Best. 'It strikes me that she doesn't seem too upset by Frank's death.'

Billy didn't speak.

'What do you think of that?'

Billy took a long drink. 'Are you suggesting she had something to do with it?'

Price shook his head. 'I'm not suggesting anything. I'm just trying to get a feel for her.'

'She didn't seem that upset. I got the impression she was more sorry for Ryan's sake than her own.'

'That's what I thought. But if that's the case, why would she cover for Dean? She surely has no allegiances to him? Unless she's been seeing him on the side. They do seem almost glued together at times.'

Billy tried to remember everything Adele had said. He imagined her fucking Dean, or Frank. Or both. He shivered. What was wrong with him?

'I think she might be scared of Dean,' he said.

'He is quite a piece of work. But you would think she'd be used to it by now, married to Frank for years. Then again Frank was the brains, Dean has always been the one willing and eager to do the dirty work.'

'What was Frank like?'

'Quiet, but dominating. A hard man, but relatively old-school.'

Billy looked at Price. 'You almost sound like you admire him.'

'Far from it. I've seen a lot of misery in people's lives brought about by that heartless bastard. But if I had to choose between having to deal with Frank Whitehouse or the Mackie boys, I'd take Frank every time.'

'Really?'

Price nodded. 'The Mackies are a whole new level of

scum. There's stuff they wouldn't hesitate to get involved in that the Whitehouses wouldn't even have considered.'

'Like what?'

Price looked at Rose. 'It doesn't matter. Let's just say that as the old guard of crooks die off and the new lot come in, I'm glad I'm retiring soon. If I can nail the Mackies for Frank's death, and Dean Whitehouse for the Mackie shooting before I go, then I'll have done a pretty decent job of cleaning up the mess in this city.'

Billy thought about that. All this from a car accident. His car accident. Maybe he'd performed a public service, starting a chain of events that would end with the criminal world destroying itself. Happy ever after. Yeah, right.

'Anyway,' Price said. 'I was hoping you might be able to do me a favour.'

'Oh?'

'Nothing drastic. I was just wondering if you'd mind going to see Adele Whitehouse again, see if you can get something more out of her.'

Billy pictured her. She said she'd phone. He slipped his phone out of his pocket and sneaked a look. Nothing.

'I don't know.'

'Rose tells me you had a fairly unorthodox way of getting to her.'

'Maybe.'

'I don't need to know the details, just the results, if you manage to speak to her.'

'I don't see what you're expecting me to achieve. You interviewed her at the station, what else can I do?'

'Judging by your piece, quite a lot. She opened up to you. Rose has a theory that it's down to animal magnetism.' He smiled at her across the table, and Billy felt like he was playing gooseberry. 'I wouldn't know anything about that. But whatever the reason, I think it's worth a go. Are you up for it?'

'I suppose.'

He wanted to see her, couldn't stop thinking about her. Something had almost happened between them. He'd killed her husband. He knew about her covering for Dean. His head ached, the lump on his temple throbbing with its own life force. He lifted his hand to it and rubbed.

'That looks nasty,' Price said. 'Have you had it looked at?'

'His brother's a doctor,' Rose said. Billy had forgotten she was there. She'd let them knock the conversation back and forth, never speaking. Sign of a good reporter. 'He took a look at it, didn't he?'

'Yeah, said it was nothing to worry about.'

'How did you do it?' Price asked.

'He wouldn't tell me,' Rose said.

Billy imagined what it would be like if he confessed, finally told the truth.

'Just a stupid drinking injury,' he said.

19

'There you go, girl.'

Jeanie stuck her nose in the new basket and thumped her tail. She stepped in and circled three times, checking everything, then she nestled down and placed her chin on her paws with a look of satisfaction.

Billy had jumped in the car and headed to the big supermarket at Cameron Toll. He took a wander down the pet aisle, Jeanie sitting in the trolley. He picked up dog food and biscuits, chewy things and squeaky toys, stainless-steel bowls, a collar and lead, the basket and blanket. A handful of treats, to put some meat on her bones.

Back home, he'd arranged all the stuff in his bedroom. Zoe didn't mind. She'd always had dogs growing up, black Labs, something Billy was jealous of. Her place in Trinity had a big garden for them to run around in, and Zoe's mum didn't have to work so was always there for walks while Zoe's dad was out cutting deals or whatever, all the while Zoe traipsing across town to George Heriot's at a cost of umpteen thousand quid a year.

Now he had his own dog. It felt good. He sat on the floor and rubbed his hand up and down her flank. He wondered where she'd come from, what had happened for her to be found wandering the streets alone. Might've been abused, or maybe she was simply lost. She was undernourished, he could see that. She was friendly and obedient, though. Maybe she recognised a fellow lost soul when she saw one.

'She's beautiful,' Zoe said.

'She certainly is.'

Jeanie opened an eye. She knew they were talking about her. Her tail flickered into life briefly then dropped again.

Zoe was sitting on the bed behind Billy. 'I'm sorry.'

He didn't look up. 'What do you have to be sorry about?'

She was stroking his neck now, mirroring his own hands on Jeanie. 'We should've reported it.'

There was a long silence. Eventually Billy spoke. 'Yes, we should've.'

'But it's too late now, you have to see that.'

'I don't want to talk about it.'

'But we have to, honey.'

'No we don't.' Billy looked up finally. 'Sitting here with Jeanie is the most peaceful I've felt since it happened. I don't want it to end.'

'Neither do I, but I'm worried.'

'Of course you're worried.' Billy looked back at Jeanie, felt the soft ruffles of her fur through his fingers. 'You should be worried. Your boyfriend is a murderer.'

Zoe stopped rubbing his neck. 'Don't say that.'

'It's true.'

'Look at me, Billy Blackmore.'

He lifted his head a little.

'In the eye.'

He held her gaze.

'You are not a murderer, got it? What happened to you could've happened to any of us, to anyone. It was an accident. We should've reported it, maybe we could've saved his life, maybe not. But it would've ruined our lives, Charlie was right about that.'

'It's already ruined our lives.'

'Not if we don't let it.' Her voice was pleading. All he seemed to hear these days were pleading, desperate voices.

'It's ruined my life.'

'You have to snap out of it.'

Billy laughed. 'That's your answer? Get over killing someone by snapping out of it?'

'Look, I know whatever I say is not going to be enough to make you feel any better. That's why I think you should take the pills Charlie gave you. He says they'll help with how you're feeling.'

'Charlie says, Charlie says.' He sounded like a little kid in a huff.

'He's only looking out for you.'

'Looking out for himself, more like.'

'How can you say that?'

'Because I know him better than anyone. He's worried I'll lose the plot and confess and put him in the shit, that's all he's concerned about.'

'That's not true. If I thought that was true I wouldn't go along with him.'

Billy looked away. 'You two seem awful friendly these days.'

'What's that supposed to mean, Billy? Come on, think about what you're saying. You need to rest.'

'And take my medicine, right?'

'It's not like that.'

'We're going round in circles here.'

He got up to leave but Zoe held his wrist.

'Remember the tartan taxi,' she said.

This was a game they played. Revisiting their first kiss. It used to cement their feelings, now it seemed like a reminder of what was lost.

She pulled him on to the bed and he let himself be drawn in. Her smell was sharper than Adele's, her skin softer and more familiar, her eyes, just different, so very different from Adele's. He tried to remember the first time, in the back of a lurid cab after some student thing on campus. He kissed her now and she responded, pushing against him, her fingers running up his neck and through the back of his hair. But all he could think about was the body lying on the road, the tick of the car engine, the sudden pain flashing across his head and down his spine. He thought of Adele as he felt Zoe's tongue in his mouth. This was an unholy mess. Pain bore down across his temples as he kissed Zoe, his hands stationary, his body stiff like rigor mortis.

Jeanie barked, an inquisitive, friendly noise. It was the first time he'd heard her bark. He pulled away from Zoe and looked round. Jeanie was standing by the bed, tail wagging, watching them.

'I can't,' Billy said. 'Not with Jeanie here.'

'So put her out the room.'

'I don't want to do that.'

Zoe shuffled across the duvet. 'Fine.' She swung her legs off the bed and stood up, staring at Billy. 'I'm going to get something to drink. I'll leave you two alone.'

She stomped out as hard as she could in bare feet and slammed the door. Jeanie jumped at the noise, her head darting round and back, ears flat on her head.

'It's OK, girl,' Billy said. 'Everything's fine.'

*

He was woken by a noise. He sat up. It was humid in the pre-dawn light. Whining and whimpering, the scratching of wood from inside the room.

He shook his head free of sleep and looked round. Jeanie was pacing in a tight circle by the bed, making a keening noise, a horrible plaintive cry.

'What's the matter, girl?'

She didn't seem to hear, just kept walking round and round. She was in a daze, head down, following an untraceable scent.

'Do you want out, is that it?'

He didn't know anything about dogs. What was she doing?

He got up and opened the bedroom door. Jeanie didn't respond, just kept walking. She bumped into the chair and headed in another direction, zombie movements, slow, deliberate. She was still making the same noise, an unsettling, primal cry of discomfort.

'What is it, girl?'

He walked over and stroked her but she didn't acknowledge him. Her tail was pointing rigidly downwards. She bumped into the bedside table and turned. Her front legs wobbled a little. That crying sound, like nothing Billy had ever heard.

'What's happening?' Zoe said, sitting up.

'It's Jeanie, something's wrong. She doesn't seem right.'

The dog made a noise as if the air had just been hammered out of her lungs, then her legs collapsed and she crumpled on to the floor next to her basket. A tremor shot through her limbs and she began convulsing, her chest heaving in and out, all four legs jerking in jolting spasms. It was like a huge electric current was passing through her body. There was a sharp whip-crack noise, and Billy saw her jaw snapping in time with the convulsions through the rest of her body. Her tongue lolled out the side of her mouth and her teeth were digging at it. Her eyes had rolled back in her head, only the whites showing.

Billy scrambled towards her and grabbed hold of her snout. He tried to pull her teeth apart, get his hand in between to stop her biting her tongue off. There was a froth of saliva along the edge of her mouth as he prised her jaws away from each other, enough to get his hand inside. Blood oozed from a wound on her tongue. Her teeth dug into Billy's hand, one set on the back, the other sinking into his palm. He held his breath at the pain. With his other hand he tried to calm her, stroked her side and head. He was talking to her, reassuring her, not sure even what he was saying, just trying to keep his voice low and calm, despite everything.

And then it was over. Jeanie's jaws relaxed and her body slackened. Her eyes cleared. She jumped up looking confused and backed away from Billy.

'It's OK, girl.' He extended his bleeding hand towards her.

She didn't recognise him.

'What's happening?'

Zoe shook her head. 'I don't know. A seizure of some kind?'

'Did your dogs ever do this?'

'No.'

Jeanie was back to padding around, bumping into things, her head and tail lowered, sniffing at nothing.

'Jeanie,' he said.

Nothing. He turned to Zoe. 'She's not responding. She can't see me or something.'

Jeanie gradually got more agitated, then began making the same noise as before, a painful and confused whimpering. As she walked, the noise got louder and more frantic. She didn't know where she was, kept bumping into things.

Zoe dug out her phone. 'I'll call my dad, he'll know an emergency vet.'

She left the room, finger in her ear, Jeanie's high wail getting stronger and louder.

As the door closed Jeanie slumped to the floor again, flopping on to her side and convulsing with her whole body. Her legs were jerking like she was sprinting along a beach after a ball. Her jaws were clacking together again and Billy grabbed a book from a bookshelf and darted over, prising her teeth apart and pushing the book in between. He pulled her body to his own and tried to hold her, comfort her. He felt the vibrations, the terrible force of it passing through his own body too, setting his nerves alight as he whispered in her ear and stroked her head, her back, down her sides. Her legs were flailing against him, thuds as her paws connected with his thighs.

And then it ended again. It was over, as if it had been switched off. Her body went limp in his arms and the book fell from her mouth as her jaw muscles loosened. She was still breathing frantically, a mix of slaver and blood dribbling from her mouth.

Zoe came back in. 'Vet will be here as soon as possible.'

'When will that be?'

'Quarter of an hour.'

'Jesus. She had another fit while you were phoning.'

Zoe knelt down and stroked Jeanie's ears. 'Poor girl.'

Jeanie jumped up again, wary of her surroundings, staggering on weak legs around the perimeter of the room.

'Did they say what we should do?'

'Just try to keep her comfortable and safe till they get here.'

'God almighty.'

Jeanie had two more fits before the vet arrived, a small one followed by the biggest yet, several minutes of convulsions and thrashing, Billy trying to prevent her swallowing or biting her tongue, making sure she wasn't near any heavy objects when quaking. He felt helpless and panic-stricken.

The vet was a thickset woman in her forties with short

fair hair, and she carried a large medical case. Billy described Jeanie's fits as well as he could. Jeanie was staggering around the room, weary and desperate, totally confused. She looked right through them as if in a trance. The vet coaxed her to sit then lie down, examined her eyes and mouth then opened her case and took out a large syringe and a vial of liquid.

'You'll need to hold her tightly,' she said to Billy.

Billy stroked Jeanie's neck. 'What's that?'

'Phenobarbital, it's an anticonvulsant. It'll control the seizures. I need to give her a high dosage to begin with, to break the chain reaction of fits.'

She expertly sucked the clear liquid up into the needle, then pushed until there was no air left inside. She put the needle down and showed Billy how to hold the dog, with her body pressed into Billy's, one hand across the head, the other holding the leg she was going to inject.

'Now hold on tight, because she'll flinch.'

Billy could feel the thin bone and sinew of Jeanie's foreleg in his grip. He could feel her heartbeat thudding against his body. Her eyes were glassy.

The vet approached with the needle and pressed it against the skin. Jeanie's leg kicked free of Billy's grasp and the needle flew from the vet's hand, past Billy's face, and landed at Zoe's feet.

The vet reached for the syringe. 'I told you to hold on tight.' She checked the tip of the needle again. 'Now, have you got her?'

Billy nodded. He was scared of breaking her leg if she kicked too hard.

The vet pressed the needle against Jeanie's leg. Billy felt the thrashing reaction from the dog, but held firm as the fluid got squeezed in, the vet whipping the needle out and quickly strapping a cotton pad against the leg.

Jeanie jumped up as Billy relaxed his grip. She backed away from the three of them, looked around her. Her tail was still pointing at the floor, but her head was raised a little, and she was actually looking at them, making eye contact. She wasn't walking, just standing still. Billy felt sick. He wanted to explain to her. He couldn't bear the idea that she thought he was responsible for all this.

The vet was already packing her bag up.

'She should fall asleep in the next ten minutes, it was a substantial dose. She might be out for up to twelve hours. Keep an eye on her, check she's still breathing and her heart rate is fine. If there are any more fits or seizures, give me a call immediately.'

She handed a card to Billy. He took it without taking his eyes off Jeanie. The dog was sniffing the air, as if sensing the electrical currents out there.

The vet scribbled in a pad. 'Here's a prescription. It's phenobarbital pills. You'll need to give her three a day. Your dog is epileptic.'

'Epileptic?'

'It's quite common, especially amongst pedigree dogs due to inbreeding. It mostly affects intelligent breeds like collies. It shouldn't be life-threatening, but you'll need to manage the condition for the rest of her life. We can monitor dosages and so forth once things have settled down. These pills have a very high rate of efficacy at controlling seizures, so she has a good chance of a long and happy life.'

Billy nodded dumbly as the vet handed the prescription to him.

'You'll get a leaflet with the pills detailing possible side effects. Look out for drowsiness and lack of co-ordination, especially in the first few weeks, although that should wear off as she becomes used to the medication. There is a longer-term risk of liver damage, but that's nothing to worry about at the moment.'

Billy's head pulsed and he felt dizzy. The vet got up to leave, but Billy stayed on the floor, the prescription limp in his hand. Jeanie came over towards him warily, sniffing the piece of paper as if it might be food.

Zoe saw the vet out.

Billy reached out for Jeanie. 'Come here.'

She leaned in and let herself be held. Billy pulled her close and buried his face in her fur, sucking up the smell of her.

20

Jeanie slept all morning and half the afternoon. Zoe got her prescription then headed to the office. Charlie was out already on a split shift. Billy switched his phone off and stayed in the darkened room with the dog, watching her chest swell with every breath, soaking up the feral smell from her body.

When she finally came round he sandwiched a pill between two dog chocolates and gave it to her. She didn't seem lethargic or confused. He wondered if she had any memory of the previous night. He fed her and gave her some water, then took her out.

The sun was still beating down on everything, bleaching the world. This weather couldn't last, not in Scotland. He headed up the Radical Road; it was like a scab that needed picking.

From up high, the heat made the Pentlands fuzzy in the distance. A low haze meant he couldn't see the Bridges. He kept his eye on Jeanie the whole time. She seemed fine. He thought about what was going on in her brain in the fizzling synapses, the surges of rogue energy. He'd spent a while earlier looking up epilepsy in dogs, but no amount of clinical blurb on the Internet could equate to the horror of watching his dog helpless and writhing on the floor.

He sucked in a deep breath and looked down. Queen's Drive was open again, cars blurring up and down past the small clump of trees.

He took out his phone, but didn't switch it on. He looked at his hands. Barbed-wire cuts, gorse-bush scars, nettle stings and now dog bites. They were fucked-up maps of his life. If only he could decode the information in those scabs and sores, maybe he could find a way out of this.

He switched his phone on. Three messages. Zoe asking after Jeanie. Charlie saying that Jamie Mackie had discharged himself post-op against the surgeon's wishes. Rose asking where he was, and telling him that the Whitehouses were having a memorial service for Frank tomorrow morning at Greyfriars Kirk.

Greyfriars, Jesus, just about the most distinguished church in the city. The preserve of politicians and public figures. That's what a life of crime got you, the most respectable send-off imaginable.

He stared at his phone. No message from Adele. His fingers moved over the keys until he heard the tone. Three rings then she picked up.

'Billy.' She was whispering.

'Hey there.'

'It's not a good time.'

'Why not?'

'Wait a second.'

He heard footsteps, muffled voices, more footsteps. He imagined Dean and Adele together, her olive skin against his pasty flesh.

'What is it?' She sounded urgent, scared.

'I wanted to speak to you.'

'Jesus, Billy, you can't just call me up whenever you feel like it. Don't you understand my situation here?'

'What about my situation?'

'What about your situation?'

Billy stared out over Edinburgh. The castle looked tiny from here, on its stumpy little throne. Below him, the bushes rustled in a light breeze.

'Never mind.'

'Look, I'm in the middle of something here.'

'I bet.'

'You have no idea.'

'Are you sleeping with Dean?' It felt as if someone else had asked it, but it was his voice all right.

'Fuck off. How dare you ask me that.'

'I'm sorry.' Billy wondered what the hell he was doing. 'I want to see you.'

'Not today.'

'Got your husband's memorial to plan?' He hated the way his voice sounded.

'As it happens, yes.'

Billy looked at Jeanie. There was something different about her. She was staying closer to him, not venturing as far amongst the grass and gorse. She was clinging to him.

'I have something to tell you.'

'What?'

'Detective Inspector Price has asked me to try and get the truth out of you about Dean's alibi for the Mackie shooting.'

'Oh yeah?' A lightness crept back into Adele's voice. Billy's heart sang when he heard it.

'Yeah.'

'Pump me for information, is that the idea?'

They were flirting again.

'Something like that.'

'Isn't that supposed to be his job?'

'He was impressed with my *Standard* piece. Thought I could get inside you.'

'Really?'

'Under your skin.'

There was a pause on the line. 'Maybe you can.'

There was noise in the background, a door banging.

'I have to go. Maybe see you tomorrow at the memorial service.'

She hung up.

He looked down. Jeanie was sniffing at his shoes, circling his legs so closely that he could feel the warmth of her body through his trousers. He knelt and gave her a hug.

21

The graveyard was a jumble of ancient moss-green stones. Morning sunlight played through the crevices as mourners in designer black made their solemn way to the kirk. Despite the sun, a dankness hung amongst the graves, hundreds of years of history weighing down the air like mist. A handful of paparazzi lurked outside the church entrance, snapping at scowling faces. Two outside broadcast vans were parked further away, reporters preparing pieces for camera.

Billy walked alongside Rose. He had Jeanie on the new lead, and she trotted along close by his side.

'I still can't believe you brought that mutt,' Rose said. 'We're working here.'

'I didn't want to leave her on her own.'

Rose shook her head. 'The great crime reporter, with Greyfriars Bobby along for the ride.'

A minister in black robes came out and pleaded with the photographers and journos to move away from the entrance. They didn't budge. The two thugs Billy recognised from the Whitehouse place came out and asked more forcefully. Everyone shuffled down the path and on to the grass.

A steady stream of mourners was still going in, the sound of camera clicks mingling with murmured conversation.

'God, will you look at them,' Rose said. 'Councillors,

businessmen, advocates. I never realised Frank Whitehouse had so much of the city in his pocket.'

'Why would they care, now that he's dead?'

'Sucking up to Dean. There's a power vacuum and the last thing these clowns want is any disruption to routine. They don't want psychos like the Mackies in charge of things, so they're showing solidarity with Dean, presuming he's going to take over the mantle.'

Billy stroked Jeanie as Rose got her notebook out and began scribbling in shorthand. His phone beeped and he pulled it out. A message from Adele. *Your name's on the list, A x.*

Billy turned to Rose. 'You'll never guess what.'

'Pope's a Catholic?'

'I've got an invite for inside.'

Rose chuckled to herself. 'From the merry widow?'

Billy nodded.

'You're some guy. I don't want to know what you and her have been up to.'

'It's not like that. I'm just keeping her sweet, as instructed by your close friend PC Plod.'

Rose narrowed her eyes. 'What does Little Miss Sunday Supplement make of you getting friendly with Adele White-house?'

Billy looked at the people going inside. Well-fed men squeezed into expensive suits, showcase wives in tight black dresses.

'Why should she mind? I haven't done anything wrong.'

'Really?'

Billy turned and held the lead out to her. 'Hold this, I can't take Jeanie inside.'

'I'm not looking after her.' Rose waved her notebook. 'Some of us are here to work.'

'Do you want me to get another exclusive with Adele or don't you?'

'Tie her up there.' Rose pointed at a nearby disabled hand-rail. 'And get some good colour for the piece while you're inside, eh?'

Billy looped the lead around the rail then bent and ruffled Jeanie's fur, comforting her. He sauntered up to the thugs at the church door and gave his name, smiling as they grudgingly moved aside for him.

He took a seat in the back pew and slunk down. He got a notebook out and started writing, just notes about the place, the people, the atmosphere. The grey stone columns, the wooden rafters, the stained glass and organ, the hubbub of expectation. None of this would get used in a *Standard* piece, but he wrote anyway to keep his hands busy. He'd been at it a couple of minutes when a hush spread through the congregation.

Dean, Adele and Ryan Whitehouse walked down the aisle to the front row. Ryan clutched Adele's hand and looked in-timidated. Adele had on the same large glasses she'd worn the first time Billy saw her. She was in a dark blouse and a figure-hugging black skirt, cut to just above the knee. She looked stunning. He couldn't see a trace of emotion on her face. Dean walked beside her, eyes cold. Billy imagined being in Dean's place, walking to the front of the church with this beautiful woman.

After they were settled in the front row, the minister made everyone rise. There were prayers and hymns, short speeches. Billy stared at the back of Adele's head as she sat through it all, occasionally dipping to whisper in Ryan's ear. Billy thought about Jeanie outside, about Zoe down in the office. He thought about Charlie in his doctor's coat, and then pictured himself and Charlie in black ties and what were then their school shoes and uniforms. White shirts and black trousers weren't the kind of thing you wore every day, so they'd had to return to dressing up like schoolboys for their mother's funeral. There had been hymns and prayers that day, but Billy couldn't remember any of it. No one made any speeches. He and Charlie weren't up to it, neither was anyone else. The minister had spouted some platitudes, then they were out of there, the tiny throng of people who knew their mum, colleagues and shop owners, precious few else. The minister wanted them out in a hurry, he had another funeral in five minutes. And that was it.

Billy realised the memorial was almost over. Dean was re-taking his seat after saying something, Billy had no idea what. They were about to rise again for a final hymn when Billy's phone went off. Several people turned round and tutted under their breaths. He grabbed it from his pocket. Rose.

'What?'

'Get outside, now.'

Billy's first thought was Jeanie. He bolted out of his seat, the echoing clatter making more heads turn. He ran for the door, vaguely aware of several more phones going off behind him. Dean's two goons weren't at the door any more. He ran out and spotted them ten yards ahead, standing over the body of a dog. A collie.

He looked at the handrail where he'd tied Jeanie up. Not there. Photographers and journalists swarmed all around, gathering around the dog's body, jostling for position, cameras out and mobiles to ears.

He pushed through them to the dog. It was covered in blood from a gaping wound in its neck. He rushed to it and knelt down, pushed his hands into the bloody fur. He was overwhelmed with relief. It wasn't Jeanie. White patch over one half of the face. Much thicker around the middle. A male, older. He let go of the body.

A voice behind him.

'Jesus Christ, is that Rebus?' It was Dean Whitehouse.

'Looks like it,' said one of his goons.

'Is he dead?'

The goon nodded.

'What the fuck happened?'

'A car drove up. No plates. Toyota. Two guys in balaclavas threw the dog out of the passenger seat and fucked off.'

'Holy shit. The fucking Mackies. Cunts. Get it out of here before the kid sees it.'

'Uncle Dean, is that Rebus?'

Billy's guts tensed at the sound of Ryan's voice.

'No, son,' Dean said.

The two heavies pushed past Billy and lifted the dog by the legs.

Billy turned. Dozens of people were spilling out of the kirk, Adele and Ryan at the front of the pack.

'It is.' Ryan already had tears in his eyes. 'What's wrong with him?'

'Nothing. Don't look.'

Adele reached for Ryan and jerked his arm, pulling him into her waist. The two heavies took the dog's body out of sight. The sound of cameras going off filled the air like perverted birdsong.

Dean turned to the snappers. 'Fuck's sake, leave us in peace, will you?'

He ushered Adele and Ryan towards a waiting car.

'Billy.'

It was Rose behind him, on her mobile and dragging Jeanie. She handed him the lead. He petted Jeanie, who was whining softly.

Rose covered the mouthpiece of her mobile. 'She went mental when they dumped the dog.' Then into the phone: 'Yes, that's correct.'

She turned away. Billy kept stroking Jeanie, pulling her emaciated body to him and sinking his nose into her fur.

'It's OK,' he whispered. 'Everything's fine.'

There was a crunch of gravel as the Whitehouse limousine sped out of the churchyard, followed by photographers clicking away.

Rose was back. 'Just spoke to the Dog and Cat Home, they got a collie in last night. A girl came to pick him up, said she was the owner. By her description it sounds like the same schemie airhead who was with Wayne Mackie at the hospital the other day.'

'Christ. Who could do that to a dog?'

'Come on, and bring Lassie with you. We've got another story to write.'

22

'I heard about what happened.'

Billy glanced up and saw Zoe standing over him, looking concerned. He nodded at his screen.

'Just finished writing it up with Rose now.'

Zoe spotted Jeanie curled up under the desk. 'You brought her into work?'

Billy stared at Zoe. 'I didn't want to leave her at home alone.'

'Maybe you should've thought about that before you got her.'

Billy pictured Adele on her doorstep, refusing to take the dog.

'Jeanie's fine, aren't you, girl?' He turned to Zoe. 'It's only until she gets used to the pills.'

He thought about the blister packs stolen from Charlie in his pocket. He was itching to take something, to feel the dry shape of a capsule in his throat as he swallowed.

'I need a piss,' he said.

Zoe tried to reach for him but he was already walking towards the toilets.

'Meet me for a coffee downstairs?' she said.

Billy stopped and turned. 'Sure. Take Jeanie with you.'

He watched as Zoe led the dog to the stairs, then he made

for the bogs. Inside he popped two morphines and two methamphetamines. He still hadn't opened the mood stabilisers. He had Jeanie's phenobarbital in his pocket too. He stared at the packet, wondered what they would feel like. He put all the blister packs back into his pocket, splashed some water on his face and stared at himself in the mirror. His skin felt waxy, as if the water had slid right off it on to the floor. He prodded his cheek, then rubbed at the bump on his temple. Was it hurting? He was having trouble telling. He cricked his neck widely and accidentally smacked his head on the hand dryer.

'Fuck.'

He stared at the hand dryer, which had gone off, blasting air downwards, noise like an aircraft engine. He banged his head on it again, deliberately this time, and harder.

The sound of a door opening. A suited guy came in, thick around the middle, shirt untucked. Billy put his hands under the dryer and rubbed them together. Pain shot through his head and palms, all the injuries talking to each other.

He yanked at the door and left.

Downstairs in the cafeteria, Zoe was sitting next to the huge glass wall at the back of the room. Outside, a couple of smokers, then across the road the arse end of the Crags, the tail of the Radical Road slashing across the hill. He couldn't escape it.

He grabbed a coffee and sat down.

'I heard you were inside the church for the memorial service,' Zoe said.

He could feel her stare, but kept his eyes on Jeanie.

'Who did you hear that from?'

'Rose told me.'

'Since when were you and Rose best pals?' Billy didn't like the sound of his own voice. Every syllable made his head throb.

'We're not. Look at me, Billy.'

He raised his eyes. It was blinding sunshine outside, the Crags in heavy shadow. A pair of gulls traced routes across the cliff face. The light outside gave Zoe a diffuse halo around her hair, her face in shade like the cliff. He couldn't make out her expression. He widened his eyes, felt air on his eyeballs. His hands were tingling in Jeanie's fur, creepers of sensation climbing up his forearms.

'Rose is worried about you.'

'She's got no need to be.'

'I'm worried about you, too.'

'I thought we established all this a long time ago. Everybody's worried about little Billy.'

Zoe sighed. 'Why are you being like this?'

'Like what?'

'Weird. Uptight. Different.'

'You know why.' Billy's voice came out loud. The sound of it sent needles into his brain.

'Calm down.'

Billy's leg twitched. Jeanie stood up and circled his chair, licked his outstretched hand, then settled again.

'I know you, Billy,' Zoe said.

He looked past her at the Crags.

'At least, I used to.'

His phone beeped. He stared at his coffee on the table, trying to make sense of the swirling patterns of steam rising off the oily surface.

'Aren't you going to see who that is?'

Billy shrugged, then took his phone out. A text. *I want to see you. The Crags pub. Now.* He pushed the phone back in his pocket.

'I've got to go.'

'What is it?'

'Got another lead on this story.'

Billy stood up and made a noise to Jeanie. She rose with a flick of her tail.

Zoe stared at him, but didn't get up. 'Was that Adele Whitehouse?'

Billy looked at her, her face dark against the glare outside.

'No.'

23

He was sweating by the time the pub came into view. Wet patches under his arms, a strip of moisture up his back, a fusty heat radiating from him. He smelled of pills and stress. When did he last have a shower?

He looked down. Jeanie was panting heavily. This stupid fucking sunshine, when would it end? It was unnatural, killing them all with cancerous shards. To his left Salisbury Crags throbbed with energy, the gorse blazing away.

The tables in the beer garden were busy. He stopped and scanned them, but no Adele. He went in, Jeanie trotting behind.

The pub was almost empty. Just two old-timers at the bar in overcoats, of all things, and Adele tucked away in a corner by the dartboard. Her bug-eyed sunglasses were pushed up on to her head, that beautiful red hair spilling out of the sides. She was frowning and fidgeting with a slice of lime in a tall gin and tonic.

She spotted him and stopped fiddling, tried to put on a calm face. She sucked the lime juice off her fingers and made an involuntary grimace.

'You came,' she said.

Billy was standing over her.

'I came.'

'I didn't know if you would.'

'Yes you did.'

'Did I?'

Billy nodded at a second gin on the table, condensation glistening on the glass.

She smiled.

'I got that on the off-chance. I figured if you didn't show, I'd manage to take care of it myself.'

She nodded at a stool.

'Just a sec.' He handed over Jeanie's lead and went to the bar. He got them to fill a soup bowl with water for the dog. While he was waiting he glanced back. Adele had her face buried in Jeanie's fur, nuzzling her and stroking behind her ears. Jeanie's tail flicked against the leg of the table. It was intimate, like a lovers' embrace. He turned back to the bar and spotted a bottle of that beetroot schnapps high on a gantry. His stomach flipped and he had to hold the bar for support.

Back at the table, he clunked the bowl on the floor and Jeanie began lapping at it, water spilling over the sides and darkening the wood.

He sat down. 'So.'

'So.'

'You wanted to see me?'

Adele looked suddenly vulnerable. 'I bet that made quite a story for your paper.'

Billy shrugged.

'You did write it up, didn't you?'

Billy nodded. Adele looked at him, her eyes glassy. She was stoned again. Always stoned.

'Rebus's throat was slit.' She gripped her glass, her fingers tense and pale. 'From ear to ear. What kind of sick fuck does something like that?'

'The Mackies.'

Adele nodded. 'That's what Dean said. Are you sure?'

Billy shrugged. 'A girl picked the dog up from the Dog and Cat Home yesterday. The description fits a girl Rose and I saw with Wayne Mackie at the hospital.'

Adele lowered her eyes. 'Dean is going to kill them all.'

Billy looked at her legs. She was still wearing her memorial outfit from this morning. Short black skirt riding up her thighs, legs crossed, killer heels.

'You have to get away from him,' he said.

'I can't.'

'He's dangerous.'

She looked up. 'You think I don't know that?'

'Just leave.'

She laughed, sarcastic and hollow. 'Just like that, yeah? He'd kill me. And where the hell would I take Ryan anyway?'

The question hung in the air. Billy didn't have an answer.

'Ryan is distraught.'

'Shouldn't you be with him?' He had no idea why he said it.

Adele's eyes narrowed. 'Who the fuck are you, the parent police? He's at home, actually, and Magda is there. I had to get out. OK?'

'Sorry.'

Silence at the table. Just the gentle snuffling of Jeanie. Billy stared at Adele's legs, her smooth calves, her manicured toenails perfect blood red. He felt his face and hands tingle, seemed to see sparkles in front of his eyes, tiny explosions of light. He scrunched his eyes shut then opened them again, but that only made it worse. He could smell burnt coffee, an overpowering aroma. He looked round the pub. The barman was standing flicking through the paper. The coffee machine was untouched.

'The police aren't sure that the Mackies killed Frank,' Adele said. 'They say their alibi seems pretty tight. They were in a club till well past Frank's time of death. Hundreds of people were in there with them.'

'Maybe they got someone else to do it. Or maybe it was just an accident.'

'An accident?' Incredulity in her voice. She sighed, a tremor in her breath. She gulped at her gin. 'I can't handle all this.'

Billy tried to reach for her hand, but she looked nervously round the empty bar and pulled away.

'Everything will be OK,' he said. It sounded weak, worse than saying nothing.

She took a deep breath and looked at him. 'I have some coke. Fancy a line?'

Billy felt his heart crashing against his ribs. He nodded.

Adele picked up her handbag and stood up, smoothing her skirt down. She swayed a little, like a breeze might knock her down.

'Meet me in the disabled toilets in two minutes. Don't be obvious.'

Billy watched her go, his eyes on the curve of her skirt. He looked round. The pub was still almost empty. The barman was the same young guy who'd been working here the last time he was in, and he was watching Adele head round the corner towards the toilets, his eyes on her body.

Billy glugged at his gin till it was just sweating ice and lime snug in the bottom of the glass. He stroked Jeanie, patted her and ruffled the scruff of her neck. He gently and calmly looped her lead around the table leg, whispering in her ear the whole time.

'I'm just going to the toilet, OK?'

She had plenty of length to mooch around. He'd be back in two minutes. He got up, cringing as his chair scraped the floor. Jeanie flumped on her haunches and scratched at her ear. She watched him walk away.

He tried to look nonchalant, his arms and legs moving awkwardly as he pushed himself onwards. He caught that burning smell again but didn't look round. His pulse was juddering as he pushed open the toilet door.

Adele was bent over the cistern, holding her hair back with one hand, smoothly snorting a thick line with the other. She used a stainless-steel straw, not a rolled-up note. She blocked a nostril and sniffed the sticky hit up as high as she could. She gave Billy a vacant stare, then her eyes widened. She switched hands with the straw, held her hair back with the other hand, and took a second hit from the coke, pulling at her nose and shaking her head afterwards.

There was another thick line of coke already chopped out. Adele handed the straw to Billy.

'Don't say anything, just do it.'

He bent and took the hit, stopping halfway to change nostrils. He felt the surge in his brain immediately. His head was a balloon full of water, ready to burst. The lump on his temple pulsing away into the cosmos. He felt his muscles and sinews stretch and tighten, his blood hammering through his arteries.

He straightened up, making guttural snorting sounds, and looked at her. She checked herself in the mirror, running a finger softly around her eye socket and over her cheek, where the shadow of a bruise remained. She leaned in over the sink, her face only a few inches from the glass. Her skirt was stretched tight across her arse. Her top had ridden up, revealing a sliver of tattooed skin at the small of her back. She produced a lip balm, smudged some on a finger and ran it across her mouth. Billy couldn't take his eyes off her.

She was smiling into the mirror. 'Like what you see?'

'You know I do.'

'What are you going to do about it?'

She smacked her lips together. It was obvious and corny, but he was sold. He edged across the room until he was standing behind her. He saw himself in the mirror, his head above hers. He looked like a wax model, inert and lifeless. She moved her arse against him and his cock throbbed at the contact. She ground against him some more. She looked desperate for something. Maybe a way out of this whole mess. But the two of them were just getting deeper into it. She lowered her hands and braced herself against the taps, pushing against him. She was looking at herself in the mirror, not him. They were both staring at her.

'Fuck me,' she whispered.

He lifted her skirt up and rubbed her panties. He moved the underwear aside and slipped a finger inside her, then two. She let out a tiny breath, like she was in pain.

'Sorry.'

She shook her head. 'No.'

He didn't know what she meant.

He unbuckled his belt and pulled his trousers and shorts down. His cock sprang up against her bare buttocks. He removed his fingers as she guided him inside her, pushing against him so that he went in deep.

'I'm so sorry,' he whispered.

'Don't speak.'

He heard the sound of Frank's body rolling over the top of the Micra. He felt his head smack against the windscreen, pain shooting through his body. He moved in and out of her as she put her hands on the mirror and lowered her head. He wanted to explode inside her, fuck the pain and guilt and bullshit away.

She lifted a hand from the mirror, raised her head and slapped herself in the face. It was a clumsy action, but hard, and her head rocked with the impact. He froze. She looked at him in the mirror.

'Don't stop.'

'But . . .'

'And don't fucking speak.'

She ground against him faster and he began again, in and out, feeling himself close to coming. She slapped herself again, harder this time, then again and again. Her hair was tangled in a mess over her face, but he could see her skin was red, her eyes wet, marks of tears on her cheeks. She kept hitting herself as he thrust against her, forcing her pelvis into the edge of the sink.

He saw something out of the corner of his eye, a red flash, darkening to purple. He turned his head, but the glimmers moved too. He suddenly felt sick, his nostrils full of the stench of burning. A searing pain pummelled across his forehead and down his side, making one side of his body convulse in shock. He caught a glimpse of himself in the mirror, his face contorted and melting, then he lost all control of his body, felt himself falling backwards towards the cold floor, his mind disintegrating into blackness and silence.

24

He stood at the top of the Radical Road, gazing out over a city shimmering in starlight, watching himself drive up Queen's Drive down below. The Micra was huge, three times a normal car size, with tracks instead of wheels and a strange glow radiating from inside. He could clearly see himself at the wheel, Zoe alongside, Charlie smacking the back of his seat, all three of them laughing.

An army of people marched down the road, not flinching as the Micra ploughed through them like a tank, crushing them or knocking them high up into the air. The people marched on into the slaughter. The figure of him at the wheel was laughing as he smashed into body after body.

Up on the cliff, he shook his head. He launched himself from the edge and flew upwards before swooping down towards the copse of trees where the Micra-tank was still creating carnage. As he got closer he saw that the people weren't random strangers, they were arranged in repeating groups – him, Adele and Ryan pulling a collie on a lead. They were smiling as they were torn apart by the vehicle, sharing a serene, angelic look which made him lose concentration and tumble out of the sky, down towards the mass of destruction below, arms swiping at the air, wind shrieking in his ears, lungs unable to breathe, heart dead, a cold stone in his chest. He hit the ground and it felt like an embrace.

Then came the pain. It didn't sweep in or sneak up, but landed like a jackhammer in his head, crushing all thought. His body stiffened with the intensity of it, every nerve ending alive with the stimulation, sending screaming messages to his brain. His brain. Pulsing and throbbing and aching, it felt as if it was desperate to escape his skull, blinding flashes across his forehead and temples, thrusting round to the base of his neck and back again, no escape.

He smelled burning. Maybe his brain frying in the pain. He heard voices. Talking about him, but he couldn't make out what they were saying. He heard a click then a few moments later received an overwhelming wash of relief, a familiar dampening down, a monumental suppression of the agony, like a glacier pushing down on the land beneath it. Morphine. Sweet fucking beautiful morphine.

More voices, drifting away as he receded into the glorious relief of a dreamless sleep.

Eventually he bobbed back up. He sensed that time had passed. The pain was still there, but like an echo of before, a repressed memory.

Voices again. Two men. He recognised one of them.

He took a slow, careful breath, as if using his lungs for the first time. He opened his eyes.

Charlie and an older man at the end of his bed. He was in hospital. White doctor coats and antiseptic. Their lips were moving but the sound was out of sync, like a badly tracked movie clip. He closed his eyes, felt the intense weight of his eyelids, then opened them again.

The older man looked at him, said something to Charlie, then walked away. Charlie turned to him and smiled. It was a genuine smile, but it also hid something.

'Hey, Bro.'

Billy tried to speak, but no sound came out. Charlie poured a cup of water and raised it to Billy's mouth.

'Here, small sips.'

Billy wet his lips and tongue, felt the cool liquid slip down his throat. He pushed away the cup.

'What happened?'

'Take it easy, all in good time. You in much pain?'

Billy felt the ghost of his earlier distress. He wasn't in pain, but he nodded anyway.

Charlie pushed a button connected to a drip in Billy's arm, and more morphine flooded his body, a thick, fuzzy glow of detachment.

Charlie sat on the bed, gearing himself up for something.

'What is it?' Billy said.

'I won't lie to you, Bro, it was fucking scary, but you should be OK.'

Charlie looked down for a second then back up.

'According to the MRI scan you had a cerebral aneurysm.'

'What?'

'It's basically when some of the blood vessels in your brain burst.'

'How?'

'Causes vary, it can be because of high blood pressure or atherosclerosis ...'

'Wait ...'

'That's high cholesterol in the blood.'

Billy's head pulsed away. He felt his throat constrict.

Charlie looked nervous. 'Aneurysms can also be caused by head trauma.'

Billy stared at him for a long time. 'The accident?'

Charlie looked around him. 'Keep it down. Yeah, maybe the accident. Could be that some of the cerebral artery walls were weakened in the knock you got. Just waiting to blow whenever you got the blood pumping.'

He looked closely at Billy.

'Speaking of which, do you remember where you were when you passed out?'

Billy closed his eyes. A mess of blurry visions swam in his mind. His face melting in a mirror. A line of white powder on ceramic, snorted up through a steel straw. Adele slapping herself until she was crying, her skin raw, hair tangled over her face.

'Yeah.'

Charlie edged closer. 'What the hell were you thinking?'

Billy shook his head.

'Fucking the widow in a pub toilet?'

'How ...'

'She did good, the widow. Got help straight away. Your pants were still at your ankles when the paramedics showed up. I've managed to keep that from Zoe. What the fuck is going on, Billy?'

Billy struggled to breathe.

'I know about the coke. Blood tests came back. I've managed to keep that quiet as well. I'm pulling in shitloads of favours to cover for you, I hope you realise that. You know the coke probably set off the aneurysm, that and the sex. Holy shit.'

Billy's lungs were full of wet concrete. Swathes of morphine still coursed through his veins, soaking into his bones, but he could already feel the smothering effects wearing off, the spectre of pain lurking in the back of his mind, ready to pounce.

'Jeanie?' he said.

'What?'

'I had Jeanie with me. In the pub. She was tied to a table.'

'While you were in the bogs snorting and screwing? Nice.'

'Where is she?'

Charlie shook his head and sighed. 'I'll find out. She's probably still at the pub. Either that, or your friendly widow took her home. She turned down the offer to ride in the ambulance with you, by the way. Probably for the best, in the circumstances, don't you think? What are you going to tell Zoe? She'll be in to visit soon.'

Billy pushed the heel of a hand into his eye socket, just to feel something.

'I don't know.'

'She needs looking after, you know. You're not the only one suffering in this whole mess. She doesn't need you cheating on her with the widow of the man . . .' He trailed off. 'This is so fucked up.'

Billy lifted a hand to the bump on his temple, and was surprised to touch bandages. Several layers of thick, rough cotton, by the feel of it, wrapped round the top half of his head. He ran a hand over his crown and down towards the back of his neck. Charlie reached out quickly and pulled his hand away.

'Careful.'

Billy felt a shiver go through him. 'What?'

'You're lucky to be alive.'

'What happened?'

'You had to undergo surgery, it was a life-threatening situation. I signed the release forms.'

'What kind of surgery?'

'The brain surgery kind.'

'What does that mean?'

'A cerebral aneurysm causes intracranial pressure. That's pressure in the brain, in the cerebral arteries, in the cerebrospinal fluid. Your brain swelled up. Basically, your skull was like a pressure cooker. That pressure had to be released.'

'How?'

'There are different ways, but you weren't responding. It was a last resort. They had to take drastic action.'

'Like?'

'That guy I was talking to before, he's a brain surgeon. He performed an emergency decompressive craniotomy.'

'Fucking hell, Charlie, in English.'

'It's a procedure where part of the skull is removed. It gives the swelling brain room to expand without getting damaged.'

Billy stared. 'You mean I've got a fucking hole in my head.'

Charlie nodded.

'Jesus Christ.'

'It's not as bad as it sounds. I mean, it's far from ideal . . .'

'You think?'

'Obviously there's a risk of infection – meningitis, brain abscess . . .'

'Whoah.'

Charlie put a hand on Billy's leg. 'Those are worst-case scenarios. Most likely they'll be able to perform a cranioplasty once they're happy that the swelling has gone down enough. They'll put a plastic plate across the opening, it's standard.'

'I have a hole in my head.'

'I know.' Charlie tried to sound reassuring. 'But chill your boots. The last thing you need is to get worked up about it.'

'That's easy for you to say.'

He felt an overwhelming nausea sweep through him, his tongue sweating, his gut roiling. Charlie spotted the look on his face, lifted a container out from beneath the bed and put it under his chin.

'That'll be the anaesthetic, takes a while to wear off.'

Billy felt vomit and bile thrust up his throat and out, splattering into the container, thick mucus dribbling down his chin. He retched two more times then took the glass of water from his brother and sipped, swilling then spitting.

'Done?' Charlie said.

Billy nodded weakly. He felt light-headed and dizzy, eased himself back into his pillows.

Charlie got up, holding the container. 'I'll get rid of this. You need some rest anyway. Try to get some sleep, I'll be back in a bit.'

Billy watched him turn and walk down the corridor of the ward. He closed his eyes and tried to ignore the throbbing sensation in his brain.

25

He was woken by the sound of coughing in the next bed. He gently turned his head and opened his eyes. A paper-skinned old man was spitting into a cup, his hand shaking, saliva dribbling down his fingers.

Billy looked round the ward. Sunshine was beaming in through the dirty windows. It felt like morning, which meant he'd been out for hours. Judging by the look of the others in the room, he was the youngest in here by twenty years. All men, mostly fat, all old. And him, with his missing piece of skull and swollen brain. Jesus.

The doctor he'd seen yesterday with Charlie came striding down the corridor like he owned the place. Tidy beard, narrow eyes, distinguished grey hair. He stopped at the end of the bed and threw a desultory smile in Billy's direction. He did that thing doctors always do, picking up the chart at the end of the bed and sucking his teeth a little.

'And how are we today, Mr Blackmore?'

Billy did a quick inventory of his body. It felt as if he'd spent a week at sea, battered by storms, eventually washed up on the shores of consciousness. Pain swarmed his body, especially his head and neck. But he was alive, breathing.

'Fine.'

'Really?'

'Yeah.'

'Don't say "fine" if you don't mean it. I have no time for pleasantries. I need to know how you feel.'

'I feel fine.'

The doctor approached him and got a torch out of his pocket. Without asking he pulled at the skin below Billy's eyes and shone the torch at him.

'Look up.'

Billy obeyed.

'You've certainly been in the wars.'

'So it seems.'

'I believe your brother informed you about the operation I had to perform?'

'Yeah.'

'You're a very lucky young man, Mr Blackmore. There are very few surgeons around here who could have performed that operation. None as good as me.'

'Even if you do say so yourself.'

'Indeed.'

The doctor checked Billy's other eye, then nodded at the bandages wrapped around his head.

'Is it worth asking you about the cause of the head trauma?'

Billy tried to smile but the muscle movement made his face ache. He just shrugged.

'You clearly got a bump on the head here.' The doctor lightly tapped Billy's temple. 'That was probably the cause. Any idea how that might have happened?'

Billy stared at the doc. Had Charlie given him a story

already? Was this guy trying to catch him out? Did he know about car crash head traumas? Maybe this was his chance to come clean.

He kept his voice level. 'Just a stupid drunken thing. Walked into a door.'

The doctor narrowed his eyes. 'And when was this?'

'A few days ago. Sunday night, I think.'

The doctor made a sceptical noise through his nose. 'Hmmm, that could explain it, I suppose.'

He put his torch away then placed both hands softly on Billy's head, like a faith healer. He began probing expertly, concentrating on the back of the skull. Billy felt his brain pulse and throb.

'One other thing, Mr Blackmore.'

'What?'

'There was quite a substantial amount of cocaine in your system.'

'Was there?'

'Don't treat me like an idiot, Mr Blackmore. I've seen things in thirty years working in this hospital that would make you puke your bowels up. For the sake of your brother, who is a very promising young doctor, I've agreed not to contact the authorities about this.'

'That's very good of you.'

The doctor gave Billy a hard stare. 'For your own sake, I very strongly recommend you stick to officially prescribed medication during your recovery period. Any other forms of stimulant or narcotic could very well kill you, in your current condition.'

'I'll bear that in mind.'

'You do that, Mr Blackmore.'

The doctor began to walk away then spoke over his shoulder. 'Presuming you don't have a relapse or infection, you could be out in a week or two.'

He was already halfway down the corridor, white coat flapping. It was only then that Billy thought to ask about when they were going to patch up the hole in his skull, but the doctor was gone.

Billy let his head fall back on to his pillows. Pain poured in now the distraction of talking had gone, and he pushed the button attached to his drip. The blanketing embrace of morphine smothered him. He wished he could stay under the surface like this for ever, disengaged from the real world and all its brutal horror.

He tried to sleep but his mind was a churning, swirling mess. This was payback. Frank Whitehouse had got his revenge from beyond the grave, placing a ticking timebomb in Billy's brain with the accident, a bomb set to go off at any minute. Ha, who was he kidding, any minute? It was set to go off at just the perfect time, the moment of sweetest justice, when he was fucking Frank's widow. Fucking the pain and guilt away, except he wasn't doing anything of the sort, because the pain and guilt had just come back a hundredfold, a millionfold, meting out its glorious revenge on him, literally blowing his mind, bursting his brain open, making it swell and expand so that they had to cut away his skull to let it breathe in peace.

Fucking karma. Why didn't he just confess right at the

start? Charlie and Zoe had talked him out of it, but it was all his fault, and his alone. He was driving, drunk and wasted. He was weak and allowed himself to be persuaded not to call an ambulance, the police, whoever the fuck could've helped.

But he couldn't confess now. He was still weak, too weak for the truth. What about Adele? What about Ryan, who had lost a daddy and a dog in less than a week? What about Dean and the Mackies? He was in the middle of a terrible shitstorm and couldn't see a way out. It would've been better if he hadn't been saved, if they'd just let his brain explode and kill him. That's what he deserved.

He suddenly thought of Jeanie. Who would look after her if he died? And where was she anyway?

He sat up and looked round. Where was his phone? A small bedside cabinet. He opened it and there were all his clothes, neatly folded.

'Hey.'

He looked up. Zoe, with a worried look. Christ, he didn't deserve her. So much better than him, stronger, more together, more focused. In control. Everything he wasn't.

'I brought someone to see you,' she said.

He noticed she was holding a lead. A snuffling sound came from underneath the bed.

'Jeanie.'

The sound of a tail thumping on the floor, then her head popped out from under the bed, ears pinned back in sheer, uncomplicated joy.

Zoe smiled. 'Dogs aren't normally allowed in here, but Charlie sweet-talked the nurses.'

'Come here, girl,' he said. She nuzzled into him. He stroked her head and tickled her chin. He rubbed her flanks, feeling the ribs still poking through the fur. He leaned down to smell her, soak her up. 'I'm sorry I left you. I won't ever leave you again.'

'You really love that dog, don't you?' There was a hint of something in Zoe's voice, a tinge of sadness.

Billy wanted to say something in reply to that, but he couldn't think what.

'Thanks for bringing her. Where was she?'

'Still in the pub. I think they wanted to adopt her. They'd made her quite at home, fed her and taken her for walks. When Charlie got back last night we headed over there and picked her up. She was upset not to see you, so I thought I'd bring her in this morning.'

'What about her medication?'

'It's OK, I've kept up with the dosage.'

'And no problems, no fits or anything?'

'Billy, I think you have a bit more to worry about than Jeanie at the moment.'

Everything she said was weighted with a strange kind of sadness. Did she know about him and Adele in the toilets?

'How are you feeling?' she said.

She sat down on the edge of the bed, far enough away that they weren't touching.

'Fine, considering I've got a swollen brain and a hole in my skull.'

'Don't joke about it.'

'Who's joking?'

She looked down at her lap. Her hands were lying there, motionless, and she stared at them as if they belonged to someone else.

'I really care about you, Billy.'

'I know.'

Jesus, was she about to dump him? He couldn't blame her.

'Charlie and I have been so worried about you.'

That 'Charlie and I' made him bristle. It sounded parental, like they were a couple. He remembered the two of them mollycoddling him, persuading him not to call the authorities, not to confess. Trying to keep him medicated and calm, under their control. Had it really been like that? He couldn't be sure, he wasn't sure about anything any more.

He felt Jeanie lick his hand, the roughness of her tongue on his skin. He imagined her licking up all the poisons that were leaching out of his pores, cleansing him of all the bad karma and drugs and nightmares.

'Everything's going to be OK,' Zoe said.

She placed a hand on top of his on the bedsheets. It was cold. She'd always had bad circulation, was always wearing more layers than him around the flat. They made a joke of her freezing extremities. Cold hands, warm heart. His own hands were hot and slippery with illness and medication and sweat. What did that say?

He leaned over to shove his nose into the side of Jeanie's head, pulling his hand out carefully from under Zoe's and tickling Jeanie behind the ears. The dog smelled of something primal but comforting. Eventually he raised his face to Zoe's. She seemed sad beyond words.

A door slammed and they jumped. Jeanie flinched and backed away, head darting around nervously.

'You fucking cunt.'

Billy recognised the voice. Here it comes, he thought, bring it on.

Dean Whitehouse was striding down the corridor towards them, finger pointing, eyes blazing, veins in his neck twitching.

Billy instinctively pushed Jeanie out of harm's way and raised his hands in a half-hearted placating gesture.

'I'm going to fucking kill you,' Dean said. 'You little piece of shit.'

He was almost at them now.

Zoe looked at Billy and got up from the bed.

'Billy?'

'Dean Whitehouse,' Billy said. 'Frank's brother.'

Zoe turned to Dean. 'Now wait a minute, you can't come in here . . .'

'Shut your fucking face, you posh bitch.'

He pushed past her and launched himself at Billy, grabbing the front of his hospital gown and hauling him up.

'I know what you were doing with Adele in the pub toilets. Fucking my brother's wife when he's not even cold in the ground. You sick fuck.'

He threw a punch. Billy didn't even try to defend himself. What was the point? He was going to die here, there was nothing he could do about it.

'Billy?'

It was Zoe. He couldn't look at her.

Dean laughed, indicating Zoe. 'This your bird? Very nice.'
He turned to her. 'Didn't you know, darling? This slimy little
cunt has been fucking my sister-in-law, taking advantage of
her grief.'

'It's not like that.' Billy wasn't sure why he was bothering
to speak.

'Billy?'

He looked at Zoe now. Tears forming in her eyes. She
backed away from the bed.

'Zoe, wait.' Why? What would he do if she stayed? He
had no words.

Dean still had a hold of Billy's gown. He threw a rabbit
punch into Billy's side, sending shockwaves through his
body. Billy struggled to breathe.

Then suddenly Dean was spread across Billy's lap, three
men in hospital uniforms pinning him against the bed and
pulling at his arms as he thrashed around, screaming, his
neck muscles and shoulders straining.

The three men lifted Dean away from the bed by his arms.
Dean grimaced, shot Billy a stare full of venom, then spat at
him. Billy felt the phlegm hit his cheek and lips and raised a
hand to wipe it off, trying to get breath back into his lungs as
he drowned in pain, soaked in it.

Dean was being dragged backwards. 'I'm not finished
with you, fucking prick. Watch your back. I'm going to destroy you.'

The men yanked at Dean, making him flinch. They pulled
him past Zoe, who stood there frozen to the spot, watching
Dean with her eyes wide.

Dean was still looking at Billy, rage in his eyes.

'Stay away from Adele, you dirty cunt. Understand?'

Everyone in the ward was staring at them. With a clatter and swish, the men hauled Dean back through the door, leaving a vacuum of silence to fill.

Zoe turned to Billy. Tears on her cheeks now, a look of understanding in her eyes.

'Wait,' Billy said, but he didn't really mean it. Why should she wait, to hear more bullshit?

She turned and strode down the corridor, raising her hands to her face, not looking back, then she was through the doors and away.

Billy stared at the doors, swinging to a stop.

He heard a whine and spotted Jeanie cowering next to the bedside cabinet.

He put his hand out. 'It's OK, girl.'

He tasted blood in his mouth, then noticed spatters of red on his white sheets.

Jeanie crept towards him tentatively, but he made comforting noises to bring her near. When she was close enough, he stroked her snout and head, making small shushing noises. He felt the tension leave her body, then he lowered himself back on to his bed, still touching her face with a limp hand.

He pushed the morphine button and kept pushing until he knew there was no more coming.

26

More drug-soaked sleep, distressed, swimming with night-mare visions, him in the pub toilets standing over Dean bent over the sink, then their faces morphing into Zoe and Charlie, then his mum frowning at him, Jeanie's simple stare, all of them crushing him, making his head explode. Images of his brain liquefying, pouring out of the hole in his skull and down the sink, everything that's him disappearing into the gutter then the sewer then out to sea.

His eyelids snapped open. His breath caught in his chest then released in a chain of sickly gasps. He felt a slick sheen of sweat all over his body, sticking him to the sheets. Then new pain sweeping in, his face, kidneys, mingling with the old pain, the familiar throbs and aches and pulses of death flowing through him.

'Are you OK, Kiddo?'

Rose. Thank fuck.

She was sitting by the side of the bed, her face was worried, full of compassion. It was good to see a face like that.

'I'm fine,' he said.

'Because you look like shit.'

He coughed out a laugh and winced, pain across his midriff and forehead.

She smiled. 'It only hurts when you laugh, eh?'

'Something like that.'

'It's been quite a week for you, huh, Kiddo?'

'I thought my nickname was Scoop.'

'You seem more like a kid than an ace reporter, sitting there in your hospital jammies, lost to the world.'

Billy looked round. It wasn't quite daylight outside, maybe around sunset, a warm evening glow ebbing through the window. He examined the ward, same spread of old-timers, wheezing and spluttering towards a bitter end.

'Where's Jeanie?'

'The dog?'

Billy nodded.

'Your brother took it home. I met him on my way in.'

Memories of his last conscious spell began filtering into his mind. Zoe. And Dean. The truth about Adele.

Rose was watching him intently. He knew she could read his face.

'What were you thinking?' she said.

'What do you mean?'

'Come on, I know what you were up to. In the toilets with the merry widow? That is quite something.'

Billy raised a hand to his face. His skin felt like a plastic bag, creased and artificial. He ran a hand over his bandaged head, trying to find the weak spot with his fingers.

'Does everyone know?'

Rose sighed. 'Not sure how far word has got out. Tom and I will keep it out the *Standard*, but I can't guarantee the tabloids won't get a sniff of it. I spoke to the barman, persuaded him to keep his mouth shut if anyone came asking, but if one of the red tops gets wind of it and offers him money, there's not a lot I can do.'

'It's not really news, though.'

'You're right, a rival reporter taking drugs and having sex in a pub toilet with the grieving widow of a recently murdered, notorious Edinburgh crime lord – not news-worthy at all. I think the worst hack in the world could make a case for that getting some column inches, don't you?'

'It wasn't like that.'

Rose stared at him. 'Look, I'm on your side. You're a friend, a colleague, OK? We cover for each other, look out for each other. And you got us some great stuff on this story, although now your means of getting the scoops looks rather unprofessional, to say the least. But anyway. Rest assured that the paper is going to do its best to protect you in all this, I have the gaffer's word. And I've got your back too, OK?'

'I appreciate that, Rose, really.'

She looked down. 'But you're going to have to take some serious time off, you understand? You're way too close to this whole thing, to the point where you're part of the story.'

Billy had a flash – Frank's body clunking up the bonnet and over the roof of the Micra.

Rose nodded at Billy's bandages. 'I guess all that nonsense will take a while to recover from anyway.'

'Brain surgeon reckoned I could be out in a week.'

'Really? Modern medicine, eh?'

There was silence for a moment, just the low thrum of hospital machinery, occasional coughs from other patients.

'Listen,' Rose said. 'Your brother told me that Dean came to see you.'

'Yeah.'

'And threatened you.'

'That's putting it mildly.'

Rose shook her head. 'I'd love to tell you not to worry about it.'

'But you can't.'

'I know what that arsehole is like, Kiddo. Maybe you should consider lying very low for a while. Maybe even leaving town.'

Billy thought about that. His dead mum, absent father. His tiny microcosm of life. 'I've got nowhere else to go.'

'No, I don't suppose you have.'

Billy's orphan status hadn't taken long to come up in conversation with Rose when he started at the *Standard*. He wasn't exactly shy about mentioning it, using it for leverage. It always helped to have sympathetic, middle-aged women on your side, taking care of the motherless child in all his sorrow.

Billy spoke. 'Zoe knows.'

Rose sighed. 'I thought she might.'

'Dean told her.'

'I'll bet he did.'

'I don't think I can go home.'

He was angling, and they both knew it. Rose played along.

'Hell, if you need a place to stay when you get out of here, I've got a shockingly uncomfortable sofa bed with your name on it.'

'Thanks.'

'Don't mention it. Just make sure and get better, OK?'

She patted his hand maternally and looked him in the eye.

'Listen, Kiddo. I wouldn't be doing my job if I didn't ask this . . .'

Billy nodded. 'Go on.'

'Did you get anything out of Adele when you met, something that might help with the story? And the case, of course.'

'You still in touch with the detective inspector?'

'Very much so. We make a pretty good team, I think.'

'He's lucky to have you.'

'Oh, please.'

Billy was surprised to see her blush. He'd never seen her blush before.

'Anyway,' she said. 'Did you get any info from Adele?'

Billy shook his head. 'It wasn't that kind of conversation.'

'I can imagine.'

'It really isn't like that. It's hard to explain.'

'You don't have to explain.'

'I feel like I do.' Billy could feel tears welling up, a hot prickle swarming over him. 'I need to talk to someone about it.' He looked down.

He felt Rose's hand on his, a loving squeeze, and tears fell. He caught his breath and sniffed, immediately wiping his eyes with the backs of his hands.

'I feel something for Adele, but it's not . . .'

'It's OK.'

'No, it's not.' Billy looked up. 'Rose, there's something I have to tell you.'

But he couldn't. Looking into her eyes, her concerned face, he couldn't talk, couldn't work out how to get his mouth to make sound. Couldn't face the awful fallout, especially not from her. She was like his mum, his memory and imagination blending them into one. His heart plummeted like an anchor.

'Don't worry about it,' Rose said. 'Women are trouble, Kiddo, you should know that by now. Best just stay away from us.'

Billy got the tears under control and put on a fake smile. 'Must be the medication making me weepy.'

'Must be. Hey, what am I thinking, I've got some news that could cheer you up. The police have got a witness.'

'The Whitehouse case?'

'Of course the Whitehouse case, what else?'

Billy put his hands on his legs, tried to stop them shaking. All he could feel was a colossal pulse in his ears, bursting to get out.

'What sort of witness?'

'A taxi driver came forward. Said he drove past a stationary car on Queen's Drive in the early hours of that morning.'

'Did he see anyone?'

'No, but that's the thing.' Rose was excited, newshound instinct kicking in. 'It was parked, no one in it, lights off.'

'So?'

'So, whoever it was must've hit Frank Whitehouse, then

stopped, got out and moved the body to the bottom of the Radical Road.'

'And?'

Rose shook her head. 'I'll blame the painkillers for your slowness, yeah? That means it wasn't an accident. If it was an accident, why not report it? Or why not just drive off? Why go to the bother of moving the body to make it look like suicide?'

'I don't know.'

'It still doesn't quite add up, though.'

'Why not?'

'The police don't think the Mackies were responsible, at least not directly. They have a strong alibi.'

'They could've got someone else to do it. Made sure they were somewhere public when it happened.'

Rose grinned. 'Now you're starting to think like my Scoop again. But the type of car is unusual.'

'The taxi driver identified it?' Billy heard his own voice catch, it was fucking obvious.

Rose shook her head. 'A small red hatchback, that's all he could tell the police. That fits with the forensics so it's definitely the car responsible. But forensics also came up with a definite age limit – at least ten years old. Something to do with polymers in the paint that are now banned or something.'

'So what?'

'I can't imagine an associate of the Mackies, or a hitman or whoever, driving around in a small, ten-year-old hatchback, can you? These clowns all have souped-up racers or executive sports numbers, not wee family cars.'

Billy felt something wash through his body, not pain exactly, but a horrible shiver, like a spirit entering him.

Rose leaned back. 'Anyway, don't you worry about it, I'm on the case. I think we're getting close to finding out who was driving that car.'

Billy closed his eyes and took a slow breath.

'You OK, Kiddo? You don't look so good.'

He pushed the button for morphine.

'Want me to get a doctor?'

He shook his head. 'Just tired.'

'Right, I get the message, I'll leave you to it. Got some loose ends to chase on this story anyway.'

Billy watched fireworks dance on the inside of his eyelids, and felt Rose's hand on his. He smelt her flowery perfume, a familiar and comforting smell.

'I'll pop back in tomorrow, see how you're doing. Take it easy, Scoop.'

He gave a vague nod of the head but didn't open his eyes.

The clack of her heels on the floor faded away, then he opened his eyes. He lifted his hands to his temples and began to push in, scrunching his face up and trying to fill his lungs with air.

27

He eased himself out of bed with small, tentative movements. Didn't feel too bad. His legs were weak but stable. His head wasn't pounding too much. His heart raced in his chest, but when had it ever not done that?

He crouched down, still attached to the drip, and opened the bedside cabinet. Shoes and socks at the bottom, shorts, jeans and T-shirt, then jacket on top. Methodical, precise. He'd never seen his clothes so tidy before.

He rummaged in the jacket pockets. He pulled his jeans out, and felt the heft of his phone. A whiff of beer and piss. That's what came from passing out on the floor of a pub toilet. He pulled the phone out. No messages.

He thought of Adele. Dean knew about him and her. He flicked through till he found her number and pressed call.

She answered after two rings.

'Billy.'

Her voice was quiet, upset. There was a sniffle and a hesitant breath. She'd been crying.

'Adele, are you OK?'

She laughed, a croaky sound. 'Shouldn't I be asking you that?'

Billy rubbed at his bandages. 'I'm fine.' His haunches were sore from crouching, so he slumped on to the floor and leaned against the bed. It felt secretive, whispering on the phone down there. 'What's the matter?'

'It's nothing.' Her voice was cracking.

'Come on, something's obviously happened. Is it Dean?'

'Did he come to see you?'

'Yeah.'

'Are you all right?'

'I'm fine, Adele, don't worry about me. It's you that's been crying. Tell me what he did.'

She burst into thick sobs, emotion crackling down the phone. He felt helpless.

'Adele, shhh, it's OK, calm down.' He tried to sound in control.

Eventually her crying settled and calmed, and she sniffed loudly.

'Just tell me,' Billy said.

Another deep breath. She was gathering herself.

'He knew I'd met you. I think he had one of his guys follow me. I don't know. I didn't see anyone in the pub. But somehow he knew.'

'What happened?'

'I was obviously upset when I got in, after you had collapsed. I couldn't hide it. He was there, interrogating me. Not just asking, demanding.'

'Did he hit you?'

'He fucking . . .' She crumpled into tears again.

'OK, take it easy, deep breaths.'

She spoke through the sobs. 'Fuck off with your deep breaths.'

'Sorry, just trying to help.'

'Deep breaths aren't going to bring my baby back.'

'What?' Billy felt part of his brain leak out of his head, his skull came crashing in on itself. 'Adele, what did you say?'

'Nothing.'

'What has he done? Is it Ryan?'

'Ryan's fine.' She was trying to regain composure. 'Forget I said anything.'

'Don't be stupid. What baby? What did Dean do?'

A long silence down the phone. Adele trying to calm down. Billy softened his voice.

'Come on, you can tell me.'

Another lengthy pause.

'I was pregnant. Just a few weeks.'

'Frank's?'

'Fuck you, of course Frank's.'

'Sorry, I didn't mean it like that.'

A different silence on the line now, simmering rage.

'Dean knew. He was so angry when I told him about us. He hit me in the stomach.'

'Jesus Christ.'

'It was only a few weeks. Just a grain of sand. But it's gone now.'

'I'm so sorry.'

Adele didn't speak, just gentle sobs.

'Adele, you have to get out of there.'

'Don't, Billy.'

'Just get out.'

'We've been through this. Where would I take Ryan?'

'I'll sort something out.'

She laughed. 'You're in hospital with a broken head.'

'I'm fine, the doctor says I could be out in a week.'

A sudden seriousness in her voice. 'Billy, you can't save us. Don't even try.'

Billy leaned forward till he was hunched over on the floor. 'I can save you.'

'Don't be ridiculous.'

'I'm not being ridiculous.'

'You're in hospital.'

'I can walk out of here any time I like.'

'You've just had brain surgery.'

'So what?'

'Billy, you have to get better.'

Billy was rocking on the floor. 'Where's Dean now?'

'What?'

'You're on the phone to me, so he's obviously not there. Where is he now?'

She sighed. 'He said he was going to deal with the Mackies once and for all.'

'What?'

'He took his little posse and headed out half an hour ago. Revenge for Rebus, that's what he said. But he never gave a shit about that dog, it's all about saving face and getting control of this town.'

'Just leave then. Before he gets back. Go to the police.'

'The police can't help. They're as scared of Dean as I am.'

'That's not true.'

'It is.'

'I'm coming to get you.'

'Don't be stupid.'

'I'm coming.'

He ended the call before she could say anything else. The phone rang immediately, but he switched it off.

He stayed on the floor for a few seconds, then carefully heaved himself up to his feet. Dragging his drip-on-wheels with him, he pulled the thin privacy curtain around his bed, checking up and down the ward as he went. There were no nurses or doctors, just patients. It was properly dark outside now and a few bedside lamps were on. Some old-timers were sleeping, their snores reverberating up and down the echoey room.

Once the curtain was drawn he leaned against the bed for a few moments then reached down and pulled out his clothes, placing them on the bed. He began to get dressed, slowly, carefully. No extra pain. When he got to his T-shirt, he realised the drip was still attached to his hand. He quickly pumped the switch a dozen times, felt the comforting swathes of morphine engulf him. He examined the drip. There was a junction where the needle fitted into a tube, with a small plastic tap attached. He turned the tap then, using his chin to keep the needle in place in his skin, he pulled out the tube leading to the drip bag. The needle stayed in place, taped to the back of his hand. Nothing leaked out.

He pulled on his T-shirt and jacket, then sat down on the bed to get his shoes on. Some coughing from a nearby bed. Sounded like the old guy was bringing something up. No sign of a nurse coming to help, though. He struggled with his shoes, his fingers clumsy with morphine and nerves. He felt sweat dampen his armpits as he finally got the laces done.

He sat on the bed for a few minutes getting his breath back, gathering himself. Then he pulled aside the curtain and peeked out. No movement. He began walking toward the doors. An old-timer glanced up at him and raised his eyebrows. Billy smiled and gave a little wave. The old guy shook his head in a 'kids today' gesture.

Billy was at the entrance to the ward. In one direction was a desk with two nurses stationed at it. He recognised them from earlier, which meant they would recognise him. In the other direction were more wards and corridors, doors leading off to other parts of the hospital. He began walking, not looking back, waiting for the nurses to shout after him. He was sweating along the edge of the bandages on his head, the bandages that were blasting out a signal like a beacon – patient escaping, patient escaping – then he was round a corner, more identical corridors and doors, people in scrubs and uniforms, patients in nighties and pyjamas, and him, striding through it all like he was completely at home, examining the stream of incomprehensible signs, hoping to find a way out.

He just kept walking and turning corners. No one stopped him or even looked in his direction. An exit sign caught his eye. He went through the doors and shuffled down two flights of stairs, then he was at the entrance of the hospital, a handful of visitors and patients outside smoking fags, a car park and bus stop across the road glowing like apparitions in the sodium light of the street lamps.

He got his phone out and switched it on. Two missed calls from Adele. No message. It was half ten at night. What day was it?

A gang of taxi drivers was standing in a huddle at the taxi rank, smoking and swapping bullshit. A thug with Hearts tattoos separated from the pack and opened the door of the first taxi when he saw Billy approaching unsteadily.

'Where to?'

He gave Adele's address.

The driver got in and examined him in the mirror.

'You OK, mate?'

'Just drive.'

The engine started and they pulled out, Billy bracing himself against the judders and rumbles that sent shards of pain snagging through his body.

28

Each speed bump made his head rattle as the taxi turned into Blacket Place. Heavy oaks leaned over garden walls, lights were on above ornate front doors. A middle-aged woman walking a golden retriever eyeballed Billy as he paid the driver and eased out of the cab.

What must he look like to her, bandaged head, zombie shuffle, wheezing for breath? He stared at her and she turned away with a tut under her breath. Lowering the tone of the neighbourhood, no doubt. That was a laugh, considering one of her neighbours was a major criminal.

The Whitehouse place seemed so peaceful, a happy suburban home. A chink of light splayed out from between the closed curtains of a front room. He scrunched up the gravel and peered between the curtains. Adele, feet tucked under her on the sofa, just like when he'd met her in the summerhouse. That was a different life, a different time, long gone. She was cradling a huge glass of red wine and staring blankly at a TV screen above the fireplace.

He tapped on the glass. She jumped and spilled wine on the arm of the sofa, then turned to the window. Her eyes widened and she shook her head vigorously. Billy pointed towards the front door. She kept shaking her head, telling him no, but she got up, glancing nervously around, then headed from the room.

. As he scuffed round to the front door, the light over the porch went off. She must've killed it. The door opened a crack.

'Go away,' she said.

'Come with me.'

She looked panicked. 'Dean's in the garage out back. He'll be in any minute.'

'All the more reason for you to leave. Now.'

'I can't. Ryan's asleep.'

'So wake him.'

'You're fucking insane. Look at you. Get back to hospital before you drop dead. And leave us alone. We're fine.'

'I'm not leaving you with him.'

She reached a hand through the crack in the door and pushed his chest. He tried to grab her wrist but missed. The shove caught him by surprise and he took a couple of steps back then steadied himself.

'Just go. He'll kill us both if he sees you.'

She closed the door in his face. He could see her walk away through the crinkled glass. He stood staring at the patterns on the glass, like raindrops running down a window.

He stepped back and gazed up at the house. No other lights on. He crept round the side of the building till he could see the garage. The door was open, a light on. Inside, Dean was pulling a sweatshirt on over his head. The two goons were there. One picked up a pile of clothes on the ground next to Dean, the other swung a petrol canister backwards and forwards. They left the garage and walked to a large metal bin like a brazier, threw the clothes in, poured petrol over them and set the whole thing alight, throwing a metal lid on top. They were laughing and patting each other on the back. Dean used a remote control to close the garage door and put the light off, then they began walking towards the back door of the house.

Billy stood looking at the metal bin, whispers of smoke curling out the side of the lid. He stood there for a long time, hearing voices inside the house, the three men joking and excited. He didn't hear Adele.

Eventually he walked away from the Whitehouse place. He turned left then left again and headed home, his bandaged head screaming like it was in a vice.

*

At the corner of Rankeillor Street he stopped and leaned against a low wall. Across the road was St Leonard's police station, where he'd passed out at the press conference. When had that been? He felt dislocated from his past, from everything that had happened before the aneurysm.

Inside the station was a police officer manning the front desk. Billy tried to picture himself walking across the road and going inside. He looked down at his feet then rubbed at his eyes, pushing his thumbs into the tops of his eye sockets until little flashes of light appeared in his vision. He shook his head and turned into Rankeillor Street.

From about thirty yards away, the Micra seemed to be

glowing. It was parked underneath a street light, lit up like an alien spaceship, signalling its presence to the universe. A small, red, family hatchback, more than ten years old. It used to be their family car.

He ran a hand from the boot over the roof and down the bonnet, his fingers feeling the grime of the city's emissions, little tiny pieces of Edinburgh's soul, emitted then gathered again, never able to leave, just like him. He brought his fingers to his mouth and sucked them, swallowing all the grit and dirt his home city could produce.

Where was the car key? Charlie had it. There were no lights on in the flat. What time was it? The pubs and kebab shops were still open, so not too late.

He got his keys out, opened the door quietly and crept inside. This was his home, but he felt like a stranger. No light. No noise except the soft pad of his feet as he walked down the corridor to Charlie's room. He stood outside for an age, staring at the grain of the wood, trying to make sense of the knots and whorls.

Eventually he pushed the door open, making sure not to let the hinges creak.

Moonlight bathed the mess in the room. Asleep in bed, peaceful smiles on their faces, were Charlie and Zoe. Her hand on his chest, cuddling in. One leg over his. Like she used to do with Billy. Charlie on his back, a bare arm hanging out of the covers and over the edge of the mattress.

Billy stood looking at them, motionless, silent. Then he inched forward till he was standing over the bed. He reached down and opened the drawer next to Charlie's head. He carefully picked out half a dozen drug packets, one at a time, and placed them in his pockets. Then he closed the drawer as softly as he could. He spotted the car key on the bedside cabinet and picked it up.

It made sense, seeing them together. He straightened up and looked at their faces. They looked happy. More than happy, they looked contented. Imagine being content with life, Billy thought. Imagine that.

He backed out of the room, then closed the door behind him and crept downstairs. As he approached the kitchen, he heard a familiar scratching of claws on the wooden floor. He opened the door and Jeanie flew at him, making a subservient, pleased keening. Her tail thumped away, hitting the door, his leg, sometimes the floor as she ducked under and round him, snuffling at his hands.

She pushed herself into him, knocking him gently on to his arse, where he sat, smiling and petting her, whispering in her ear, stroking her and pulling her into a hug that was too strong, too forced, but he did it anyway.

After a while he got up, opened a cupboard door and pulled out a can of dog food. He opened it and emptied it into Jeanie's bowl on the floor, then refilled her water dish. As she scoffed at the food, he knelt down beside her.

'I'm just popping out for a bit, I'll be back soon.'

She swished her tail as if she understood. He headed back upstairs and out the front door, careful to close it without any noise.

He stopped at the Micra. He opened the driver's door, felt

around in the sun visor, then pulled out the picture of him, Charlie and their mum at the beach. Happy families.

He locked the car door, slipped the photo into his jacket pocket, next to his hammering heart, then walked down the street.

*

The bell for last orders rang just as he stepped through the door of The Montague. He drew stares from the regulars and off-duty cops. His bandaged head and shuffling gait made him feel like an ancient mummy, like he'd been dead and entombed thousands of years ago and recently been jolted back to life.

The image of Charlie and Zoe swam in his head. He felt numb, didn't even know what to think about it. He should be furious, enraged that his brother and girlfriend were sleeping together. But it was his fault. He'd been obsessed with Adele, with the accident, with the aftermath. He probably still had those mood stabilisers on him somewhere. How would things have panned out if he'd taken them? Pointless thinking about it now, everything was fucked beyond measure, beyond redemption, beyond words.

The barmaid gave him a look as he ordered a pint of Stella, then she went to pour it. He scanned round the pub, enjoying the stares from everyone, returning them intensely, smiling to himself as every one of the locals turned away under his gaze, not wanting to engage the lunatic with the bandages, the laboured walk and the hollowed-out look in his eyes.

He glugged at his pint and did an inventory of his body. He was weak and fragile, like his body was made of cracked glass. His skull hammered like a drum. He ran both hands over the bandages, probing, prodding. The bandages were tight and thick, several layers stretched over the skin like a second skull. Then he found it, the hole, a tiny bit of give in the material under his hands, in a place he didn't expect. It wasn't near the bump at the front of his head, nor on the top, but at the back, a couple of inches down from the crown, just above where the skull connected to the top of the spinal column. Why there? If he ever met that brain surgeon again, he would ask him. He thought about taking the bandages off. Getting some fresh air into his brain, with the germs and pollution and evil afloat on the breeze contaminating his thoughts. At least they didn't smoke in pubs any more, he couldn't get passive brain cancer. He screwed his eyes tight. His neck hurt. He cricked it violently, producing a loud crack that made the barmaid wince from several feet away.

'You all right, love?'

'Fine.'

His heart thudded in time with the pulsing in his brain. His organs felt bruised and battered, his liver and kidneys struggling to keep his body pure and free from poison. His hands tingled, a strange kind of electricity passing through his fingers like his whole body was a lightning conductor. He realised the needle was still taped to the back of his hand.

He pulled it out without thinking. A small spurt of blood emerged from the vein. He sucked it clean, pushed the tape down over the wound and put the needle in his pocket. He pushed at his cheeks with his fingers. His face was numb.

He pulled out a drug blister pack from his pocket. Oramorph. The clue was in the name. Morphine. He popped three and swigged them with lager. The barmaid stared at him, so he stared back.

'Migraine,' he said flatly.

He pocketed the blister pack and took out another. Pervitin. The clue wasn't in the name. Sounded like a perv's drug. But he knew it was methamphetamine. Balance out the morphine. Keep him on an even keel. He popped three and downed them. His tongue tingled, and the slide of the pills clogged his throat. He wondered for a moment what it would feel like to be drug free. He would probably die. He had no idea how much of anything he'd taken in the last however long it was, and that went for the hospital medication as well. But he felt alive for now, that's all he could hope for.

He was suddenly aware of a ringing in his ears. Couldn't be the pills working already, could it? It kept going, penetrating his brain through the hole at the back of his paper-thin skull.

'I think that's your phone, love,' the barmaid said.

He stared at her. Was she talking to him?

'Your phone?' She nodded at his pocket.

He followed her gaze. Put his hand in and pulled a phone

out. Charlie. His big brother Charlie. Interesting. He answered the call.

'Where the fuck are you?'

Billy imagined Charlie throwing on clothes, Zoe waking behind him, asking what was going on.

'I'm here.'

'Where's here? I just got a call from the hospital saying you've gone AWOL.'

'I'm in the pub.'

'Fucking Jesus. You've just had brain surgery, for Christ's sake, you should be in hospital recuperating.'

'I didn't like it in there.'

'So fucking what? I don't like it in there, but I go to work anyway. Which pub are you in?'

'I'm fine.'

'I didn't ask how you felt, I asked which pub you were in. I'm coming to get you and taking you back to hospital straight away. I hope to fuck you're not drinking. Not on top of the morphine and the surgery. Christ.'

He took a hit of his beer to wind Charlie up, making an obvious smacking sound with his lips as he swallowed.

'Billy, this is a life-threatening situation. Can't you get your head around that?'

'I'm touched by your concern.'

'Stop being a complete prick and tell me where you are.'

'The Montague.'

There was a pause. Billy savoured the thought of what was going through his brother's mind.

'The Montague?' A note of caution in Charlie's voice.

'Yeah.'

'You've been back to the house, then?'

'No, came straight here.'

Billy imagined he heard a relieved sigh down the line.

Charlie seemed to get a sudden burst of energy.

'Right, don't fucking move. I'm coming to get you. Don't drink any more lager.'

'You'll need to hurry, they've rung last orders already.'

'You're something else, Bro, you know that?'

'Oh, and Charlie?'

'Yeah?'

'Bring Jeanie with you. I want to see her.'

'Look, we're going straight to hospital . . .'

'Just bring her, or I'll be gone when you get here.'

*

They'd rung the bell for closing time when Charlie pushed the door open. He was pulling Jeanie reluctantly on the lead, but when she saw Billy she sprang forward to greet him. After an initial hug, she began snuffling around the floor, licking up crisp crumbs and whatever else she could find. He rubbed her and she looked up at him. It seemed to Billy it was a look of devotion and uncomplicated love. A look so unlike anything any human had ever fired his way.

Charlie got to the bar, shaking his head.

'I can't believe you did this,' he said. 'How did you get out of the ward anyway?'

'Just walked and kept on walking.'

Charlie let out a laugh. 'Holy shit, Bro.'

Billy lifted his pint glass to his lips and finished the dregs.

'You really shouldn't be drinking,' Charlie said.

'This from the man who self-medicates every night out.'

'I'm young, fit and healthy, you're recovering from an aneurysm and brain surgery, and suffering post-traumatic stress.'

'I'm not going back to hospital.'

Charlie tilted his head and raised his eyebrows. 'Yes you are.'

'No.'

'I promised Zoe I'd make you go back.'

'Ah, Zoe.' Billy leaned against the bar. 'How is she?'

'I know she found out about you and the widow from Dean. She's upset, how do you think she is? But she still cares about you.'

Billy looked at Jeanie, now settled in a comfortable heap at his feet.

'Look, I'll go back to hospital, but I want to take Jeanie for a walk first.'

Charlie frowned. 'Don't be stupid, I can do that once you're back at ERI.'

'No, I want to do it. Come with me.'

Charlie was about to argue but Billy was up and walking towards the door. He clicked his fingers. Jeanie got up and followed him. Charlie shook his head and made after them both.

29

Billy panted with every upward step, sweat slicking his fore-head, the bandages on his head itchy and tight.

'This is crazy,' Charlie said.

He'd moaned and complained all the way from the pub. Past the Commie Pool, down the road, across the round-about away from Queen's Drive and up the hill.

'You have to get back to hospital, Bro, I'm not fucking joking when I say this could kill you.'

'I know, you're only concerned for my health.'

Charlie stopped behind him. 'Don't say it like that. I am.'

Billy didn't stop or look back. 'I know you are.'

Jeanie was up ahead sniffing around the gorse at the edge of the path, nose to the ground, following a hidden scent.

'I know what you're doing,' Charlie shouted after Billy. 'It's ridiculous. We all went through it, not just you.'

Billy stopped with a sigh and looked back down the path.

'Have you ever been up the Radical Road before?' He nodded up the slope.

'You know I haven't.'

'Well, come on.' Billy turned. 'It's a nice view.'

Charlie stood for a moment then followed his brother up the hill.

'Fuck's sake,' he said under his breath.

He caught up in a few strides, Billy still doing a slow shuffle forwards, trying to catch his breath.

'Please come with me to hospital.'

'Stop asking me,' Billy said, determination in his voice. 'I will once we've done this.'

'Done what, exactly?'

Billy didn't answer.

They trudged on in silence. It was still light enough to see where they were going, even at one o'clock in the morning. Crazy Scottish summertime. The heat of the day still simmered over the land, refusing to leave completely. It was never like this. The weather couldn't last, it would break soon. There wasn't a breath of wind, the closeness bringing earthy smells to Billy's nose, clogging his mind. He was on the alert for that burning smell, the one that seemed to indicate a seizure or whatever it was on the way. That and the flashes in the corner of his eye. He felt tremors ripple through his body as he thought about it, anticipation of the big one, another wave of blood into his synapses that would end it all.

The path flattened as they reached the top and Billy stopped for more rest. The solemn cliffs to their right were dark, solid witnesses to all his stupidity. The slope down to their left was as dramatic as ever, tangles of gorse blossom seeming to hum in the thick air. The sky was a viscous violet, occasional stars punching through the blanket, faint glimmers from a time before human struggle.

'It's beautiful up here,' Billy said. He eased himself on to a large rock, feeling the uneven stone against his buttocks. 'So peaceful.'

Charlie stared at Billy as he tried to get comfortable on the rock.

'You're really suffering, aren't you, Bro?'

Billy rubbed at his bandages and smiled, but kept looking out at the city.

'You noticed?'

There was only the faint shush of traffic up and down the streets running south out of the city centre. Occasionally a car or taxi would sputter up Queen's Drive, moving down a gear as they ploughed up the slope, past the small clump of trees where it happened, shifting back up a gear and away as they levelled off and headed for the roundabout.

Billy found his attention drawn by them. He couldn't take his eyes off the headlights, the spreading lances of clarity that struck out from the front of each car, cutting through the half-light, paving the way for a tonne and a half of metal and plastic to power along, hoping nothing would get in the way.

He was aware of Charlie watching him as he gazed at the road, but couldn't drag his eyes away. He was unable to control himself. He had been unable to control himself ever since it happened.

'We fucked up,' Charlie said.

Billy was engrossed in watching another taxi chugging up the hill far below.

'I said we fucked up.'

Billy held his breath until the taxi had passed the copse of trees.

'Yes, we did.'

He raised his eyes to stare across the city again. The castle looked fake, like a toy fort.

'I'm sorry,' Charlie said. 'Is that what you want to hear?'

The arteries of traffic and people that criss-crossed the city glimmered yellow, carrying life and hopes and fears in every direction. Billy wondered what it would be like, to be down there with them. To be part of something again.

Charlie moved round until he was standing in front of Billy. Jeanie was snuffling somewhere over near the cliffs behind, he could hear her.

'Look at me,' Charlie said.

Billy slowly turned to look at Charlie's face. It was hidden in shadow, dark crevices around the eyes.

'I'm sorry.'

Billy stared at his brother's face for a long time.

'So am I.'

He looked down. Charlie was only a couple of feet away from the edge. A hundred feet of scree and gorse behind him.

'I don't know what I was thinking,' Billy said. 'With Adele.'

'You weren't yourself.'

'Zoe must hate me.'

'She doesn't hate you.'

A hard shove to the chest now would be murder. Charlie would never survive the fall.

'Have you talked about me?'

'Of course. We've been worried sick.'

'I guess she was upset after she found out about Adele.'

'Bro, you have no idea. She was in a total state.'

Billy couldn't see his brother's eyes properly, just dark pools of shade.

'But you calmed her down?'

'What are brothers for?'

Billy felt a smile spread on his lips. 'Good question. What are brothers for?'

'Looking out for each other, that's what.'

Billy could tell from the way Charlie's facial muscles tightened that he was smiling too. Two brothers, having a heart to heart, smiling away.

'Especially me and you,' Charlie said. 'Since Mum and everything.'

Billy narrowed his eyes, trying to look at Charlie's face, but the thin light made it impossible to make anything out.

'If I can't trust you, I can't trust anyone,' he said.

'What's that supposed to mean?'

Billy looked down at Queen's Drive, a small car plugging its way up the slope towards the trees. Someone heading home after a great night out, home to bed, to sleep and wake tomorrow refreshed.

Billy remembered Charlie with his arm round Zoe, both of them naked in bed. The contented looks on their faces, not a care in the world.

He turned to his brother.

'Tell me honestly, Charlie. Did you feel a pulse on Frank Whitehouse?'

Charlie put a hand on Billy's shoulder. Billy's arm and chest muscles twitched.

'I swear to God I didn't.'

'Swear on Mum's grave.'

'I swear on Mum's grave I thought he was dead.'

'Anything else you want to tell me?' It was as if someone else had said the words, but they came out of Billy's mouth.

'Like what?'

'Like anything.'

No talking, just the rumble of the city at Charlie's back.

Far off to the left, Billy noticed something out of the corner of his eye. Smoke. Impossible to tell the source from here, it was a few miles away, but a steady column of black was billowing up into the lilac spread of sky. Billy thought he heard the distant wail of sirens.

Charlie still hadn't spoken. Billy felt the weight of his injuries pressing down on him, crushing him. His eyelids drooped and he raised an unsteady hand to the bump on his head. It didn't seem to have gone down at all since the accident. When was that? He'd lost all sense of time. Maybe he would have the lump on his head for ever, a permanent reminder.

'We need to get you to hospital,' Charlie said.

Billy had his head in both hands now. 'You didn't answer my question.'

'What question?'

'I asked if you had anything else to tell me.'

Billy raised his head. Charlie's hand was still on his shoulder.

'No,' Charlie said. 'Nothing.'

Billy put his hand on Charlie's wrist and gripped tight.

He still couldn't make out his brother's face properly. Over his shoulder in the distance the smoke was still coughing upwards, and Billy thought he saw a flicker of flame licking the rooftops down there. Just a sliver.

'Do you think I should try to make it up with Zoe?'

'I think you should get back to hospital right now, or it won't matter a fuck what you do.'

'That's not an answer.'

Billy's grip tightened on his brother's wrist. He felt sick as he glanced behind Charlie and down the steep slope to Queen's Drive.

'I don't know what the hell you should do.'

'I'm asking your advice. As my big brother.'

'I think you should worry about it once you're better.'

'And when will that be? It feels like I'll never be better.'

Charlie placed his other hand on top of Billy's.

'Look, Bro, you've suffered post-traumatic stress and serious injuries. You need to lie down and do nothing for as long as it takes to press the reset button on your life.'

Billy let out a laugh. 'Press the reset button? Switch me off and back on again, yeah? See if I manage to reboot?'

'If you like.'

Billy felt himself squeezing his brother's wrist. Charlie's other hand was covering his, and Billy felt his hesitation.

'You have no idea what it's been like for me.'

'Of course . . .'

'My brother and my girlfriend betraying me.'

'What?'

A thudding silence.

'You both persuaded me to leave Frank in the road when I was going to report it.'

A loosening of the tension in Charlie's grip. He let out a breath.

'I'm not going over all that again.'

He lowered his hands.

Billy felt the electrical circuit broken, their link to each other severed.

Charlie turned side on, looking to the south of the city.

'Looks like something's burning, out near The Inch.'

Billy looked at his brother's outline, thick against the sickly shimmer of street lights beyond. He had never been able to fight his brother. Never been able to win, at least. Bigger, stronger, smarter. The closest thing to a dad he'd ever had.

He gazed at the drop directly beneath them, his blood thumping in his skull. He felt something wet against his hand. Jeanie's tongue. Jeanie nuzzled in for comfort and he grabbed her emaciated body and held on to her. He squeezed her until she writhed out of his grasp and mooched away to a nearby bush.

Something clicked in Billy's head.

'Did you say The Inch?'

Charlie turned. 'Yeah, around there anyway.'

Billy got up and stood next to his brother. The smoke was obvious now, spreading up into the night, thinning out and diffusing into the ether. The tips of flames occasionally licked above the roofline.

Billy gazed at it for a second, then pulled his phone from

his pocket. He made a call and waited. Four rings, then a pick up.

'Rose?'

'Billy? Jesus, it's the middle of the night.'

'I'm up on the Radical Road . . .'

'What are you doing there? You've just had brain surgery.'

'It doesn't matter. I have a question for you.'

'You're supposed to be resting.'

'I know. Just one question. Where do the Mackies live?'

'What's that got to do with anything?'

'Just tell me.'

He heard a yawn, a sigh. 'Walter Scott Avenue.'

'Is that in The Inch?'

'Yeah. Why?'

Billy thought of Dean and his goons. Burning clothes, petrol canister, laughing and joking.

He stared at the smoke, fingers spreading out above the city.

Charlie was looking at him with a confused frown.

'I think our story just escalated again,' Billy said.

30

Two dozen neighbours stood watching as firefighters clumped about in their heavy gear looking busy. There were three engines blocking the street, each with a couple of men directing a hose at different parts of the sixties pebble-dashed house that was already half demolished by the flames pouring through window frames and doorways. The flashing lights from the engines mingled with the bonfire to create an unearthly glow, like a party in purgatory.

Some of the neighbours were in pyjamas and nightgowns, others in clothes they'd thrown on. There were lots of kids, smaller ones clinging to parents, older ones in groups laughing and mucking about. This was clearly the most exciting thing to happen to Walter Scott Avenue in a while.

Billy parked the Micra and climbed out. He got suspicious stares from nearby. Not one of the locals. A nightshift news hack and a photographer that Billy recognised were standing close to the engines, one soliciting quotes from anyone he could find, the other snapping away for tomorrow's paper. They probably wouldn't realise the significance of who the owners of the house were, but they'd get told when they got back to the office.

Billy kept away from them. He wasn't supposed to be here. He was meant to be in hospital. But this was his story, he was all over it, everything about it had seeped into his blood-stream and infected his brain.

He shook his head and cricked his neck. Shafts of pain everywhere. He swallowed two painkillers and two uppers then leaned against the car for a moment. Jeanie was in the front passenger seat, shuffling around in the tight space, tail flicking, eyes bright with the reflection of the fire.

Rose had thanked him for the information and told him in no uncertain terms to get back to hospital. Charlie had told him the same thing. He'd agreed with both of them and walked slowly back down the Radical Road, Jeanie close to him, Charlie alongside, the three of them in heavy silence.

Outside the flat, Billy said he didn't want to go inside in case he saw Zoe. He didn't want to face up to that. Charlie said he understood, and ducked inside to pick up the car key to drive Billy to hospital. As soon as Charlie was in the door, Billy scurried to the Micra, bustled Jeanie in, started the engine and pulled out. His hands trembled on the wheel as he imagined slamming into a parked car, or simply not stopping at the end of the street, ploughing across South Clerk Street into the kebab shop over the road.

He turned left and headed south. He followed the plumes of black smoke, down Minto Street and past Cameron Toll, until he was at The Inch. Didn't take long, but his phone rang four times. Charlie. Fuck him. Brothers looking out for each other. Like fuck.

Now, standing in front of the Mackies' torched home, he wasn't sure why he'd come. Maybe just out of guilt. It was his fault this had happened. It was all his fault. But so what?

These weren't exactly nice people, they were violent psychos and criminals. It was good that their house burnt down, one less vipers' nest in the city.

He scanned the crowd, looking for Wayne or Jamie Mackie. Come to think of it, he'd never actually seen Jamie in the flesh, only his mugshot in several of the *Standard*'s recent stories. But he had shotgun wounds to his leg and arm, so he should be easy to spot.

There were plenty of the Mackies' type hanging around, zigzags in their hair, lurid gold chains, expensive chunky white trainers, muscles on show, air of arrogant cockiness.

He spotted the girl. The one who'd been hanging around with Wayne at the hospital. She was standing nearest to the blaze with a couple of other girls, none of them much older than eighteen, if that. She was twirling a strand of hair around her finger with one hand, taking pictures with her phone.

He walked over, his feet unsteady as he pushed himself away from the car. Behind him, Jeanie nudged at the glass of the passenger window, keen to follow.

'Where are Wayne and Jamie?' he said.

She turned. He saw a tongue piercing glinting in the flames. The heat from the building was intense here, and he felt like clawing at the itch under his bandages, scraping away the scalp underneath.

'Who the fuck wants to know?'

She looked at him side on with big brown eyes, like she was posing for a Facebook profile. Used to being looked at.

She was pretty but it was hidden, layers of make-up, sharp fringe, baggy top and micro skirt, big hoop earrings.

'I'm a friend of theirs.'

'Like fuck you are.' She laughed. Her two pals turned and began scoping him.

'OK, I'm not. But I met Wayne at hospital. After Jamie got shot. You were there.'

She examined him closely through her hair.

'Looks like you should be in hospital yersel.'

She glanced at the top of his head. His hand came up and smoothed over the bandages, from forehead to crown to nape of the neck, over the hole that seemed so natural now.

'Yeah, you could say that.'

The girl tilted her head. 'I remember you from hospital. You were there with some old tart.'

'Yeah.'

'You a reporter, like?'

'Kind of.'

'What does that mean?'

'I am a reporter.' Billy pointed at his head. 'But I'm supposed to be on sick leave.'

'So what the fuck are you doing here?'

'Just interested.' He turned to where the firefighters were struggling to subdue flames lashing the house. 'That is the Mackie place, yeah?'

The girl didn't say anything.

'I take it the lads weren't inside?'

The girl rolled her eyes and shook her head. Her pals'

attention drifted away, they were now making lewd comments and speculating about the firemen's cocks.

'Any idea where they are?'

She shot him a dagger look. 'Even if I did, I wouldn't tell you.'

'Of course not.'

Billy glanced at the house. The blaze was tearing at the roof now. The place was being gutted, it would have to be knocked down. Everything ruined.

He turned back to the girl, who was still half facing him, as if not quite rejecting or ignoring him. He took that as a cue.

'I reckon you might have the number for one of the boys in that phone of yours.'

'I might. What of it?'

'Fancy giving it to me?'

'You trying to chat me up?'

'The phone number.'

'I don't think so.'

She smiled as she gave him a withering stare. He smiled back.

'What about for money?'

He almost laughed at the reaction. She was suddenly more alert, like a deer startled in the woods. She tried to cover it, too late.

'What kind of money?'

Billy pulled out his wallet and opened it. Just a few tenners. He counted them out, showing her.

'Fifty.'

'Fuck off.'

'It's all I have.'

She turned to look at the blaze. She lifted her phone and took a picture of the flames. Without turning, she spoke.

'Go on, then.'

She was holding her other hand out, down at her side, where her friends couldn't see.

'Number first.'

She looked sideways at him. She was pushing buttons on her phone.

'Look at this picture.' She spoke loudly, for the benefit of her mates.

She handed him the phone. On the screen it said 'Wayne' then a mobile number. He memorised it, then passed the phone back to her.

He slipped the money into her open hand. She deftly tucked it inside her bra, her back turned to her mates.

Billy got his own phone out and punched the number into the address book before he forgot it.

He looked up. The girl had moved away. She was swapping derisive snorts with the others, all of them throwing looks his way.

'What's your name?' he called out.

'Fuck you.'

'It was you who picked up that collie from the Dog and Cat Home, wasn't it?'

She gave him a blank stare.

'I dunno what you're talking about.'

'You know what the Mackies did to that dog, don't you?'

There seemed to be a flicker of something in her eyes.

'Look, just fuck off, will you?'

He gazed one last time at the burning house, then turned and walked back to the car.

31

With his mind blank and Jeanie licking his hand, he flicked to the number. Pressed 'call'. Stared at the steering wheel listening to the ring. The sound was muffled through the bandages over his ear. Sounded like he was deep underwater, trying to make contact with the surface.

Five rings then an abusive answer-machine message. He hung up. He stared out the window. The firemen were beginning to get the blaze under control, but the house was a wreck of sodden, burnt wood and plaster, charred masonry, wisps of burning debris fluttering up into the sky, plumes of black smoke winking out the stars.

What would he do if someone destroyed his home and everything in it? What would the Mackies do?

He noticed the crack in the windscreen. The one Rose had pointed out all those days ago. It was bigger now, or was he imagining it? No, definitely bigger, not just a small crystal star, it had grown into a sword shape with one long blade pointing down towards the bonnet, indicating the place of impact. If he didn't do something, the whole windscreen would split eventually.

He called Adele. That same submarine buzz in his ear, as if his brain was swimming in syrup. Five rings then her recorded voice. He hung up.

The crack in the windscreen seemed to be growing in front of his eyes, dancing in the flickering light from the blaze. He reached out and touched it, imagined pushing his fists through the glass to the outside world. There was a sting of electricity in his fingers at the feel of cold glass. He examined his hands. The palms were a mess of scars and scabs.

He turned the key and the engine coughed into life. Mum's reliable old banger, still going after all this time. At this rate it would go on for ever, outlive him. But he had to get that crack fixed. When all this was over, he would do it then. Look after Mum's old car.

His hands were shaking as he touched the steering wheel and the handbrake. The engine's stuttering life mingled with his own. He pictured Frank Whitehouse lying in the road, crimson in the tail lights. The car revved and jolted as he threw it into gear and turned round, heading back towards town.

The traffic lights seemed to sparkle and shift as he drove, the headlights of each approaching car dazzling and hurting his eyes, like staring at the sun. He concentrated on his hands touching the wheel. He hunkered down and blinked out at the night.

It wasn't far to drive. Weird to think these two families lived so close to each other, yet in such different neighbourhoods. One mixing with solicitors and councillors, the other with scum, one at the top of the pile, the other trying to get there. Separated by less than a couple of miles in the Southside of a city that had perfected the us-and-them society. One dead man, one shooting, one slaughtered dog, one torched home. And more to come.

He turned into Blacket Place. Dark, quiet. No one on the street. He parked across the road from the house. Switched the engine off and listened to the ticking of the metal as it lost heat.

Jeanie had her nose in his lap. He stroked her a few times, felt the ribs.

'Stay here, girl.'

He opened the door and she shot out, scrambling across him in a fluster and darting across the road. She was squatting for a piss by the time he locked the car door. He clicked his fingers and she came, then he turned into the White-houses' drive.

The same room light was still on, the curtains closed. As he approached he realised that the front door was wide open. He stopped. No activity, no sign of life. Just an open door.

He walked up the steps to the doorway and stopped. Peered inside. Nothing. He stood for a moment listening to the pulse in his brain. Jeanie sniffed at some plants by the door.

Then he heard something. A scrape and a muffled thump. A voice, a female voice. Not talking, not crying out, but something else, an insistent kind of moan. The sound drew him inside as if mesmerised. He stood in the hallway and moved his head to work out where the noise was coming from. Damn these stupid bandages over his ears. He heard the clack of Jeanie's claws on the floor, then it stop as she reached the rug. He listened again for the noise. There, to his

216

left. It was coming from the room. The door was closed and light seeped out from underneath, splaying short fingers into the hallway.

He walked towards the door. The noise got louder. Definitely a woman moaning. In distress. He swallowed hard and put his hand on the doorknob. Turned it slowly and pushed. Stepped warily into the room.

Adele.

She was lying on the floor, on her side, tied to a chair with some kind of electrical cable. She was facing the other way, so she hadn't seen him. He looked round the room. No one else. Everything seemed normal except for a table lamp lying on the rug next to a glass of spilt red wine.

Billy scurried over and touched her on the shoulder. She squealed, flinching away from his touch. She whipped her head round and her eyes widened. She had something stuffed in her mouth, gaffer-taped in place.

'It's OK,' Billy said. 'I'll untie you. Hold on.'

She increased her efforts to speak, but Billy couldn't make out anything.

'Wait,' he said.

He ripped the tape off her face and pulled at the material till it came out of her mouth. Socks. She gasped and wheezed, sucking in air and working her jaw. She had a wild look.

'They took Ryan. They came in here and beat me up and took him.'

The Mackies. Billy didn't need to ask.

'We have to get him back,' she said.

Billy fumbled with the knot at the back of the chair, the thick rubberised cable claggy in his sweaty palms. It seemed to take for ever, his hands trembling and slipping. Eventually he loosened the knot.

Adele whipped her hands out and began working on the knot around her ankles. She pulled it free then rolled away from the chair and clambered to her feet. She swept her hair back from her face. Billy saw bruising around her eyes and cheeks, a trickle of blood from her nose.

'Are you all right?'

'Never mind me, I have to get Ryan.' Her voice was fragile, close to breaking. Billy wanted to reassure her, but no words came.

'I don't know what to do.' She talked fast, as if to herself. 'They said no police or they'd kill him. This is all about Dean. They said he set fire to their home.'

Billy nodded. 'I've just come from there, it's gutted.'

'This is crazy. Why are me and Ryan even mixed up in this?'

'I said you should've left.' He regretted it as soon as the words were out of his mouth.

She stared at him. 'Is that supposed to help?'

'Sorry, fuck. I don't know what I'm saying. I didn't mean it like that.'

'This is all for Dean's benefit. He was supposed to come home and find me.'

'Where is he?'

'How should I know? Him and those two pricks went out, probably to one of his stupid brothels.'

'What else did the Mackies say? What do they want?'

Adele was shaking her head, her whole body shivering. Billy wanted to wrap her in his arms, feel the warmth of her against him, smell her hair.

'They just said this had to end. They'll be in touch. Billy, what if they hurt him?'

She started crying, thick, heavy sobs. She gasped for air between, hands to her face, covering the bruises.

Billy put a tentative hand on her arm. 'It's OK.'

She shook him off. 'Don't say that, it's not OK. I don't know what to do.'

Billy stared at her, the light in the room too harsh, everything too sharp. Jeanie poked her head in the doorway then went away again. Billy tried to get his brain to work, tried to cajole the amphetamines into firing his neurons.

'I'm going to sort this,' he said quietly.

She stared at him like his head had flipped open.

'How the hell are you going to do that?'

Billy lifted out his phone. 'I have Wayne Mackie's number.'

'So? Are you going to ask politely to have Ryan back?'

Billy shook his head and looked at his phone. It was half two in the morning.

'When did the Mackies leave?'

Adele was exasperated. 'I don't know, maybe quarter of an hour ago.'

'I have a plan.'

'You're out of your mind. It's got nothing to do with you, this whole thing.'

'It's got everything to do with me.'

'How do you figure that?'

Billy stopped for a moment. Considered. 'It just does. Do you trust me?'

'I hardly know you.'

He moved towards her, put his hands on her shoulders. She let him. He looked at her beautiful eyes, red from crying. Her beaten face, already swollen and discoloured. She didn't deserve any of this. No one deserved this. Except him. He tucked a loose strand of hair behind her ear.

'This looks fucking cosy.'

Billy felt Adele's muscles flinch at the voice. She jumped back from him and turned to the doorway. Billy turned too, already knowing what he was going to see.

Dean and his two morons were standing in the room, faces flush with booze. Dean took in the upturned chair and electrical cabling like a snake on the floor.

'What the fuck is going on?' He spoke to Adele, pointing at Billy. 'And what the fuck is this cunt doing here?'

Adele ran over to him, stopping before touching him, wary.

Dean and the goons were eyeballing Billy.

'The Mackies have taken Ryan,' Adele said.

It took a second to filter through, Dean switching from aggressive to outraged.

He stared at Adele as if she was talking a foreign language.

'Wayne, Jamie and a third guy. They tied me up and beat me, then took Ryan out his bed and left.'

Dean looked at the chair again, the cable, Adele's discoloured face.

'When was this?'

'Quarter of an hour ago,' Billy said.

Dean turned on him. 'What the fucking fuck has it got to do with you?'

Billy felt suddenly weak and his knees began to buckle. He stumbled but caught himself before he fell.

'I came to check on Adele. I found her in here tied to the chair.'

'You must have a fucking death wish, coming round here,' Dean said. 'You look halfway dead already.'

Billy felt lightning searing through his head, making him close his eyes and scrunch his face up. Just keep going, Billy boy. He opened his eyes and thought for a moment he saw a red flash in the corner. He snorted air into his lungs, searching for a burning smell, but nothing. He felt like sleeping for a hundred years, just closing his eyes for ever. But he had to keep going, had to see this through. Just a little while longer and he could rest.

He looked at Adele. He could still fix this. She needed him. No one had ever needed him before. It felt good. He rubbed at the lump on his forehead then scratched at his sweat-soaked bandages.

The sound of ringing. The house phone. On a table next to the sofa.

Dean walked over, keeping an eye on Billy. Adele followed in his wake, staring at the handset. 'Dean,' she pleaded. 'Just do whatever they want.'

He raised a warning hand. 'Let me handle it.'

He picked up, didn't speak. Listened for a moment.

'You cunts are dead, you do know that?' His voice calm and even.

More silence, his face giving nothing away.

'Yeah, well, you started it.'

Gap.

'Don't give me that fucking horseshit.'

It was like he was conducting a business deal. The goons were eyeing him intently.

'Of course I know it. Why there?'

Pause. More silence in the room. Billy looked at Adele, her face full of fear.

'OK.' Dean hung up.

Adele grabbed his hand. 'Well?'

Dean shook her off and walked to the door. Adele grabbed him.

'Dean, what did they say?'

'We're going to meet them, get Ryan back.'

'Now?'

'In an hour.'

'Where?'

'Up Salisbury Crags.' Dean stopped and turned. 'I think it's those cunts' idea of a joke. They want to meet above where Frank's body was found. Fucking dickheads. We're going to be ready for 'em, though.'

'What are you going to do?'

'What do you think? We're going to destroy those cocky little shits.'

'But they'll have Ryan with them.'

'Don't worry, he'll be fine.'

Billy heard his own voice. 'Maybe you should go easy on the violence and concentrate on getting the boy back.'

Dean rolled his eyes. 'Are you still fucking here?' He turned to his thugs. 'Throw him the fuck out, and make sure he gets the message not to come back.'

Billy backed away and raised his hands as the two guys grabbed him and hustled him towards the doorway.

'Leave him,' Adele said, without much conviction. 'He's only trying to help.'

Dean grabbed her arm. 'Want to go with your fucking boyfriend, or want to come with us to make sure your son stays alive?'

The taller of the two goons threw a light punch into Billy's kidneys, enough to make him cry out and make his legs buckle. They carried him between them, his shoes scuffing the floor as they dragged him out of the front door and threw him down the steps. He landed in a cloud of gravel dust, slamming his back off the ground, knocking the air out of his lungs.

The two men sauntered down the steps and began kicking at him, mainly around the fleshy parts, his arse and legs, his stomach. He curled up into himself and covered his head with his arms, wondering if his skull might burst with the strain.

Before he knew it they were done. Only a dozen or so blows. Just a warning. He ached all over, struggled to get air into his lungs. He felt familiar waves of pain course through his body.

'You heard the boss,' said the shorter guy as he straightened his jacket and spat on the ground. 'If we see you again, you're a dead man, you hear?'

Billy managed to nod as he attempted to get up. He wondered where Jeanie was, if she was still in the house.

He turned and looked about. The two guys had already gone back inside and closed the door. The night was sickly and warm, the air a thick blanket over everything. He strained his ears. Eventually he heard a familiar snuffling and turned to see Jeanie cowering by the front gate.

'It's OK.' He got on to his knees, wheezing.

Jeanie stepped forwards, a tentative shuffle, tail flickering. She approached and nuzzled him, and he held on to her body, gripping the fur and the skin underneath too tightly.

He turned and looked at the house. All quiet, like a normal suburban home. No sign of danger. He let go of Jeanie and slowly pushed his knuckles into the gravel, trying to lever himself upright.

32

He drove without thinking. His hands shook on the steering wheel. He couldn't find the gear, the retching of the engine making his teeth clench.

Jeanie hunkered in the footwell of the passenger seat, looking up at him. He patted her briefly then returned his hand to the gearstick.

The streets were empty. In a couple of weeks this place would be rammed with tourists and performers for the festival. Now it was desolate, hardly another car on the road. It was about this time of night that they'd driven home up Queen's Drive.

The car seemed to drive itself. Right at the lights, down the slope past Pollock Halls, left at the roundabout, left again.

He was on Queen's Drive, heading the opposite direction from that night. Thick moonlight smothered everything. The Crags on his right glistened, the gorse bleached in the light, throbbing with life.

He slowed and pulled over opposite the trees. No cars in either direction. He kept the engine running, yanked the handbrake on. Stared out at the tarmac. No sign of blood anywhere. He wondered if it had been washed away. But there had been no rain, only incessant sunshine for days. Maybe forensics cleared it away.

He opened the car door, motioned for Jeanie to stay put, and got out. Closed the door. Stood holding the handle, staring at the view. From here you could see the *Standard* offices, Dynamic Earth, the top of the parliament building. Right in the thick of things, yet the middle of nowhere.

He let go of the Micra door and walked slowly across the road. Stopped before he reached the pavement. Just stood there on the road.

As he crouched down he felt his body and brain complain at the motion, every sinew and synapse on fire. He rubbed a hand across the rough surface. Small pebbles moved underneath his fingers.

He fell on to his knees and put both hands on the tarmac. Rubbed them backwards and forwards, then began scratching with his nails at the surface, tearing at the ground until his nails were ragged and his fingertips bloody and raw. He slumped forward, so that he was on all fours, and choked on a sob as it came out, followed by more, caught breath and tears.

Dizziness overwhelmed him, then he was suddenly sick, vomit splattering on the ground between his hands, tears still coming, his ribs heaving with the force. An animal noise rose from his gut, a primitive wail of pain caught between sobs as he stayed there, struggling to breathe.

He imagined a car sweeping round the bend and smashing into him, tearing flesh from bone, smashing his skull and brains and spraying them across the road. Leaving nothing behind, just an almighty mess.

There was a scratching sound. Jeanie's claws on the inside of the car window. He looked up and outward. No cars coming, no signs of life. He spat on to the road surface and wiped his mouth and eyes. Tasted the salt of tears and something else. Blood. A thin trail of snot and blood was running from his nose. He wiped it away with his sleeve.

He struggled to his feet like a wounded dog and staggered back to the car. There was a jolt down his arm as he pulled at the door handle. Jeanie darted across to her seat as he slid in next to her. He yanked the door closed and stared out the window at nothing.

The engine was still running. He imagined exhaust fumes filling the car. He stared at the crack on the windscreen. He would fix it. He would fix everything.

The car stuttered into life as he put it in gear and pulled away.

*

He parked outside the flat and switched the engine off. Jeanie recognised where they were and began fussing to get out. He reached over and opened the passenger door and she tumbled out in a mess of legs and fur, springing across the pavement to the tiny garden.

He sat in the car and wiped blood from his nose. It hadn't stopped. Still just a trickle, though. He went into his pocket and pulled out the picture of him, Charlie and Mum, rubbed a thumb over his mum's face, then his own. Then Charlie's. The memories wearing away. He raked through the pills in his pocket. Took two uppers and two painkillers.

He pushed open his door then jumped as a passing taxi fired its horn, swerving to miss the outswinging door. An angry voice shouted at him, then the taxi pulled away.

His pulse hammered against his skull as he eased himself out the car and locked it.

Jeanie was sniffling along the wall as he opened the front door of the flat and went inside.

The sound of a television.

In the living room, Charlie and Zoe were both asleep. Charlie was sitting up, empty beer bottle in his hand. Zoe was lying across him, head in his lap, thin blanket over her. Charlie's other hand was resting on Zoe's hair. They were both peaceful.

He lifted the remote and switched the television off.

Charlie stirred. He dropped the bottle with a quiet clunk on the carpet, then jumped at the noise. His eyes sprung open and he saw Billy standing over him.

'Billy, fuck. Where were you?'

Billy tried to remember. 'I had a story to cover.'

Charlie snatched his hand away from Zoe's hair as if he'd had an electric shock then began shaking her, pushing her off his lap.

'Zoe, Billy's home.'

She took a moment to shake the sleep, then threw off the blanket and stood up.

Billy shied away from her.

'You need to get to hospital,' she said. 'Please, Billy.'

'Holy shit,' Charlie said. 'Is your nose bleeding?'

Billy took a step backwards.

Charlie got up and reached towards him. 'Let me see.'

Billy moved away, shaking his head and wiping blood on his sleeve. It seemed like more was dripping out now, he kept catching a taste of it on his lips. He touched the back of his head, but the bandages seemed dry over the hole.

'The Mackies have kidnapped the Whitehouse kid,' he said. 'Dean Whitehouse torched the Mackies' home, so they kidnapped his nephew.'

'That has nothing to do with you,' Charlie said.

'How can you say that?' Billy felt like screaming. He clenched his hands into fists, feeling the raw skin pulsate with pain. He tasted more blood, wiped at his nose.

'I'm calling an ambulance,' Zoe said.

'Don't.'

'You could die.'

'So?'

Zoe looked at him pointedly. 'I don't want you to die.' She pulled out her mobile and dialled 999. 'Ambulance, please.'

'I won't get in it.'

'You will,' Charlie said.

Zoe was on the phone. 'Yes, my friend has had a head injury . . . No, he's conscious, but bleeding . . .'

Friend. Billy liked that. Not boyfriend. Or love of my life. It was friend now.

He felt his nails digging into the palms of his hands.

Zoe was struggling on the phone.

'. . . no, we don't know how he injured his head . . . you don't understand, he was in hospital already . . .'

Charlie grabbed the phone from her.

'His name is Billy Blackmore. He was admitted to ERI yesterday after suffering a cranial aneurysm, and he underwent an emergency decompressive craniotomy, then stupidly walked out of the ward when he woke up. We think he's suffering a relapse.' He waited a moment. '15 Rankeillor Street. Thank you.'

He handed the phone back to Zoe and spoke to Billy.

'Now sit the fuck down and don't do anything that'll kill you.'

'It's too late for that.'

'Don't be such a drama queen.'

'Come on,' Zoe said, 'please sit down.'

'I'll stand.'

Billy imagined them all pointing guns at each other.

'I know about you two,' he said.

They stole glances at each other and Zoe looked down.

'What about us?' Charlie said, faking bluster.

Billy tilted his head, felt his brain lurch.

'Don't treat me like an idiot. I saw you together in bed.'

'That was a mistake,' Zoe said. 'I'd just found out about you and Adele. I was confused and hurt, and Charlie . . .'

'And Charlie was there to take advantage.'

Zoe shook her head. 'It wasn't like that.'

'Yeah, fuck you, Bro,' Charlie said with a snarl. 'At least I was here for her. Where the hell have you been since all this started? Screwing the widow, that's where. Which, by the way, is some seriously fucked-up shit, considering what you did to her husband.'

'What I did?' Billy said. 'I thought we were all in this together, wasn't that the line? All for one and one for all? Looking out for each other?'

'We are looking out for each other . . .' Zoe said.

'Don't give me that shit. It's always been you pair trying to stop me from landing you in it.'

'Billy . . .'

'It's fine. It's good that you're screwing each other, at least now it's all out in the open. You two have each other and I'm surplus to requirements, right? Only it's not quite that easy, because I'm finally going to come clean about it all.'

'That's a bad idea,' Charlie said.

'Why? Because you'll get struck off for stealing drugs from the hospital?'

'You'll go to prison,' Zoe said.

Billy stared at her. 'I dare say those posh twats you work with won't look kindly on you fleeing a murder scene in which your boyfriend was driving, everyone loaded off their faces.'

Charlie took a step towards him, and he backed away. Jeanie picked up on the atmosphere and came to cower behind Billy's legs, making him stumble.

Charlie held out a placating hand. 'You need to sit down and cool off until the ambulance gets here, Bro.'

Billy shook his head and took another step backwards. He was edging towards the door, Jeanie shuffling behind him.

'I really don't. What I need to do is go and make everything right, put an end to all this.'

Zoe was rooted to the spot. 'Charlie, don't.'

Charlie didn't look at her, kept his eyes on Billy.

'I can't let you walk out of here and ruin your life,' he said. 'Or end your life. Anything physically or emotionally stressful could cause another aneurysm, a fatal one this time.'

Billy felt a smile curl his lips. 'So you can't stop me, otherwise you're risking my life.'

'Don't test me.'

Zoe sounded frantic. 'Charlie, Billy, stop it, please.'

'Listen to her, Bro,' Charlie said. 'Stop right there.'

'You listen to her, she's your girlfriend now.'

Billy was almost at the doorway of the room. He heard his blood singing in his veins, screaming to get out. He felt Jeanie's soft body still behind him, her presence comforting.

'Where are you going to go?' Charlie said.

'There's a police station at the end of the road, how about that for starters?'

'How do you think Mum would've felt, her golden boy in prison?'

Billy laughed. 'You were always her golden boy, Charlie.'

Charlie shook his head. 'Either way, you're going to get convicted, I'm going to get struck off. Some Blackmore legacy, eh?'

'If that's the way it has to be.'

'It doesn't.'

Billy stopped just past the door frame, standing in the hall. Jeanie scuttled to the front door, looking back anxiously and whining. Billy started walking backwards towards the door. Charlie and Zoe followed him into the hall.

'Billy,' Zoe said.

'There's nothing you can say, either of you, I've made up my mind. A boy's life is in danger because of me. I have to make it right.'

Billy was almost at the front door.

'I can't let you leave, Bro,' Charlie said.

'Then you'll have to stop me.'

He lunged for the door and flung it open, Jeanie slithering sideways out of his way as he tried to move his legs.

A clatter from behind knocked him to the ground and pushed the air out of his lungs. He felt the familiar weight of his brother on top of him, a lifetime of being smothered and crushed. He sensed the warmth of Charlie's breath on his neck. He jerked his head backwards, wincing as his skull connected with Charlie's face. Blinding pain in his head, his brain screaming. He heard Charlie gasp and felt his hold loosening. He pushed himself up on to his hands and knees violently and felt Charlie swing off him, heard a thud on the floor, but before he could turn a fist hit him on the side of the head where the lump was, more pain, a flash in his vision, then another punch to his liver doubled him over and Charlie was on top of him, sitting astride, blood and snot dripping from his nose on to Billy's face, making him spit it away.

Charlie was holding his arms, pinning them to the floor.

'You fucking cunt. After everything I've done for you.'

'Fuck you.'

Charlie backhanded him, a soft warning not intended to hurt, but everything hurt now for Billy. Breathing, thinking, being alive, it was one long stretch of agony.

There was a growl, a feral, guttural rumble from Billy's right. He and Charlie both turned to see Jeanie launch herself and sink her teeth into Charlie's upper arm.

Charlie screamed and removed his hands from Billy's arms, trying to grab Jeanie's jaws and separate them, shaking his arm to get her off.

Billy threw his fists, connecting first with Charlie's ear then with his chest. His brother made a sound like a balloon deflating and sank back. Billy pushed himself out from underneath, Jeanie still snarling and holding on to Charlie's arm.

Billy caught a glimpse of Zoe standing in the hall a few feet away, tears in her eyes, a distraught look on her face. He scrambled upright, took a swing and landed a foot in Charlie's stomach, doubling him over, Jeanie pulling at his sleeve as he crumpled.

Billy caught Zoe's eye. He stared at her for a second, waiting for something, but nothing came.

He stepped over Charlie's prostrate body.

'Come on, girl.' He pulled Jeanie away from Charlie. There was slobber all over Charlie's T-shirt, the material ripped, a trickle of blood running down his arm.

33

Billy ran, Jeanie alongside him. His stride was erratic and he stumbled as he went on, but he kept running down the street, his heart thumping, his head pounding, his body aching and complaining, Jeanie right there next to him, tail wagging, looking up at him with big eyes.

'Good girl,' he said between gasps.

He kept on running, his lungs on fire, his legs heavy with every thudding step. Straight past St Leonard's police station and up the cobbled lane that rose behind it to a tiny street. He turned the corner.

All quiet. He stopped and sank to his knees on the pavement, tried to gulp air into his heaving chest. He spat on the ground, it was black and slick. Blood. His own, maybe some of Charlie's. He wiped his nose and it came away thick with blood and mucus.

He slumped on to his arse, his breathing slowly returning to normal. Jeanie fussed over him, in about his arms and legs, looking for attention. He gave her a tight hug.

'Thank you, girl.'

He checked the back of his head. A damp patch on the bandages over the hole where he'd backwards headbutted his brother. His hand came away more pink than red, not like blood at all. What liquids were inside your skull? He popped two more Pervitin and a couple of Oramorph. Had to stay together a little longer.

Just over the rise in the road was Salisbury Crags, looming over him. The Radical Road slashed a faint line across its face, splitting the cliff from the gorse.

It was so warm, even in the middle of the night. It felt like he was breathing smoke, not air, the molecules clinging to his throat and lungs, scorching his insides.

He stood up and looked at his phone. Half three. The Radical Road filled his vision.

Not much time. Not much time left at all. He stood in silence. Jeanie sat down on the pavement and began scratching herself.

He looked at her, then at the phone still in his hand. Flicked through the menu till he got to Rose. Took a deep breath. Pressed 'call'. Brought the phone to his ear.

Five rings. Answer-machine message. Long bleep. Deep breath. Steady voice.

'Hi Rose, it's Billy, your favourite trainee crime reporter. Listen, I have something to tell you. Hold the front page, and all that.' He coughed out a laugh. 'This is all going to sound insane, but everything I tell you in this message is true. I'm sorry. You trusted me, and I let you down. Big time. This story we've been working on, the Frank Whitehouse thing, you were right when you said I got too involved, but you don't know the half of it . . .'

He rubbed a hand over his bandaged head, from the lump on his temple to the damp indentation at the back of his skull.

'OK, so I just need to tell you everything. I don't know how much time I have.'

He probed at the bandages over the hole in his head. It felt invasive and comforting at the same time. His fingers came away damp.

'Anyway, when I finish, you're going to have the biggest front-page scoop of your career, I promise you that.'

He gulped in air, found his throat sticky, struggled to swallow.

'Right, here goes. I killed Frank Whitehouse. I was driving the car that hit him on Queen's Drive that night. My mum's Micra. A red family car, more than ten years old, see? The same car I gave you a lift in the next morning. That crack in the windscreen you spotted, that was where his body hit. Zoe and Charlie were in the car too, but I was driving. We were all drunk and wasted. Charlie steals drugs from hospital and we all take them. I can't remember what we'd taken that night, but I was out of it. I shouldn't have been driving, I know that. There's no excuse. I'm not trying to make excuses.'

Billy wiped snot and blood from his nose, then tears from his eyes.

'We stopped. Frank was lying in the road behind us. I wanted to call for an ambulance or the police, but Charlie and Zoe talked me out of it. We were all in shock. Charlie checked the body and thought he was dead. Charlie's a fucking doctor, so I didn't argue. A taxi came up the road. We panicked and carried his body off the road, rolled it down the embankment, then tumbled down ourselves. I was lying next to Frank.'

He tried to catch his breath, feeling the words pour out of him at last.

'Except it turned out he wasn't dead. We didn't know that then. We left him there, got in the car and drove home. God, that was so fucking stupid. I don't know why we did that. OK, that's not true, I know exactly why we did it. We did it to save ourselves, to save our skins. But I've been living in hell ever since. Going over and over everything that happened. And, of course, to make matters worse, you called the next morning about the jumper. It was Frank, but he wasn't where we left him. Which means he wasn't dead at all. Maybe we could've saved him. He must have got up and walked away, then collapsed again.'

The tears felt like release, like a levee bursting and letting the floods wash everything away.

'I should've told you. When I saw Frank's body. I should've told you a million times that it was me, but I didn't. I don't know why not. I was lost. I've been lost since it happened. That bump on my head, that was from the accident. The aneurysm, I guess that was payback. For killing Frank, for all that crazy shit with Adele. Jesus Christ, Adele. What the hell have I done to her? This is all so fucked up.'

He stared at the Crags, dominating his sight, ghostly in the moonlight, towering over the city.

'So everything that's happened has been down to me. Jamie Mackie getting shot, that dog getting killed, the Mackies' house burning down. Adele was pregnant. She lost the baby.

And now the Mackies have taken Ryan Whitehouse. Adele's boy. They're meeting Dean soon.'

He felt hollowed out, an empty wooden statue, rotten on the inside.

'I'm going to crash the party. Up on the Radical Road. Try to get Ryan back. I have to do something. If I don't see you again, Rose, thanks for everything you've done for me. I can't explain what I've done, except to say that I never meant anyone any harm. But that's a useless thing to say. I'm sure you'll have fun piecing all this together. I wish I could help you with the story, but I suspect that one way or the other I won't be around.'

He looked up and down the street. Complete silence.

'One last thing. If I don't . . . can you look after my dog? She's been pretty good to me. Thanks, Rose, and take care.'

He ended the call and checked the time. Twenty to four. He switched the phone off and turned to Jeanie, who pricked up her ears.

'Come on, girl.'

34

He stood teetering on the edge.

His head reeled, as if his brain had shaken free of its moorings. The gorse below seemed to sway like rolling ocean swells, but there was no wind. The bandages over his ears made everything muffled. The far-off lights of the city were gauzy and diffuse, like a fogbound dream. But the sky was clear, impossibly distant stars blinking through the spread of sky, black then violet then sapphire on the horizon where the sun was preparing to rise.

The city looked like Toytown. The cliff he stood on was just a pimple on the landscape. Everything in too much perspective.

He looked around. He was surprised neither gang was here yet. Made sense to arrive early, get the jump on the opposition.

He was still struggling to get his breath back after walking up the slope. He felt like his body was floating above the ground, drifting through life. The painkillers, no doubt, all that fucking morphine. He shook his head, felt his brain rattle. Was that his imagination? The patch on the back of his skull was still damp. He suddenly wondered what the surgeon had done with the bit of skull he'd removed.

Jeanie was doing her usual sniffing routine around the

edge of the gorse, tracing the movements of dogs from earlier in the day, or other invisible scents. He'd toyed with the idea of leaving her behind, she had no business here, but where could he have put her? He couldn't go back to Rankeillor Street and he had nowhere else. He hoped Rose got his message. He smiled as he pictured her face when she heard it.

He looked down to the start of the Radical Road. Nothing. He waited to see car headlights on Queen's Drive, but there were none.

He heard voices. Harsh accents. The Mackies. The voices were coming from behind him. He turned and crouched, almost falling over the edge of the cliff, grabbing a handful of grass and dirt as he steadied himself.

Just appearing over the rise were three figures, slouched in the semi-darkness. Of course, the Radical Road went all the way round Salisbury Crags. He'd forgotten all about the other end because he'd never had reason to come that way. There was a way up from Holyrood Park, the Mackies must've used that.

Billy clicked his fingers and Jeanie came to him. He held her collar and scurried across the path, the Mackies still a good distance away. He pressed himself against the base of the cliff, in a shadowed crevice, and knelt down. He calmed Jeanie and stroked her back and sides, quietly shushing her. He made sure he held her collar with as much strength and conviction as he could muster.

The Mackies slowed as they approached the highest point in the road. The path spread out into a wider plateau at that point, an obvious place for the meeting.

Billy risked sticking his face out for a glimpse. The brother he'd met, Wayne, was nonchalantly swinging a sawn-off shotgun, talking in a constant murmur. Another man dressed in a shell suit was resting on crutches, leg bandaged, occasionally talking back to Wayne, a lit joint hanging from his mouth. Jamie. A third man, much bulkier and thicker, stood a little apart, holding on to the shoulders of a small boy. Ryan.

Billy imagined stepping out from the darkness, striding over and grabbing hold of the boy, dragging him away from all this. He pictured getting a shotgun blast in the chest for his trouble.

He tried to see Ryan's face. He remembered first meeting him in the summerhouse, the green haar of grass smoke and the evening sun giving the boy a halo as he came in looking for his mum. Who is the strange man with Mummy? Good fucking question, little guy.

He couldn't see Ryan's face now. The boy wasn't struggling, didn't seem upset. A five-year-old taken from his bed by strangers in the night. The big guy's hands gripped Ryan's shoulders in a stance that seemed uncomfortable for both. Neither of them moved. Jamie continued to drag on his joint, cradling it in the cup of his hand. Wayne shuffled his feet and waved the shotgun with agitated movements, providing a low running commentary that Billy couldn't make out.

In the distance to the left, Billy saw lights. The clunk and thunk of car doors. Voices, getting louder.

Here we go.

He pulled Jeanie closer and edged back into the crevice.

He saw four figures trudging up the slope.

Wayne stopped fidgeting to watch, and held the gun against his leg.

The four figures approached. They were silhouetted against the purple sky, easily distinguishable. Adele, Dean and the two lumps of meat. So there were three psychotic hardmen against three psychotic hardmen, Adele, Ryan, Billy and Jeanie stuck in the middle. Fantastic.

They slowed and stopped talking as they spotted the Mackies. Dean at the front pulled out a handgun and pointed it at Wayne. In a synchronised movement, Wayne pointed the shotgun at Dean.

Adele broke rank and ran towards Ryan.

'Hey,' Wayne shouted, stepping in her way with the shotgun raised.

She stopped, hands to her face, sobbing. Dean spoke quietly and one of his thugs gently pulled her back.

They were talking, Dean and Wayne. Billy couldn't make it out, he was too far away. Guns were waved, heads cocked, fingers pointed. Behind them, everyone was standing waiting. Ryan was now struggling against the grip of the big guy, Adele shaking as Dean's goon held her back. Jamie casually flicked his roach over the edge of the cliff and pulled out another joint.

It seemed like Billy was watching it with the sound and contrast turned down. The drugs made his vision foggy, the bandages echoing back the sound of his own pulse in his ears. He screwed his eyes shut and opened them again, but it all seemed blurry, floaters drifting and jerking across his eyeline.

He strained to make out what Dean and Wayne were saying, but could only hear burble and static, like a radio stuck between stations.

He let go of Jeanie and felt around the back of his head. He scraped his broken nails against the bandages, and eventually found a starting point. He picked at the loose end until it came away, gummy against his fingers, but peeling off all the same. He pulled and felt little resistance as the bandages unravelled. He looped his hands round his head, feeling the release of pressure with every sweep, his skull relaxing, his brain breathing. Four, five circuits of his head and he had most of the white gauze off, the warm air of the night fresh against his scalp.

Then the bandages were off. He bunched them into a ball and dropped them on the ground. He ran his fingers through his hair. There was a large shaved patch at the back. He felt around the edge of the area, his heart hammering in his throat, his pulse so loud he thought they all must be able to hear it, everyone across the city must be deafened by it.

He felt air at the back of his skull.

His fingers moved lightly across from the hair to the shaven scalp, then suddenly there was nothing solid beneath his touch, just skin against skin, no support, like pushing at the hollow of his cheek. The skin was still there. He'd presumed it would be gone, just a big gaping hole in his head, open to the elements. But there was still a skin flap. As he fingered it, he realised it was loose. Had they sewed him back up or not? Either way, it was loose now. That was the source of the leak. Blood leaking through the edges where the skin didn't quite meet up.

He felt suddenly alive. As if he'd just broken the surface after months under the sea. His ears were full of noise now, a rushing sound he couldn't account for. He still couldn't hear what Dean and Wayne were saying. They stood a few feet from each other, hands moving, mouths opening and closing. No one getting angry, it seemed. Not yet, anyway.

Billy looked at Adele then Ryan. He felt a surge of something through him, moving down from his head and radiating out through his body to the surrounding area. Immense energy.

He straightened up and came out of the shadows, walking as calmly as he could towards the scene in front of him, ready to interact with the world. It felt like he was walking on the deck of a ship in a storm, and he put his arms out to steady himself.

Everyone turned.

Dean shook his head. 'Jesus fucking Christ.'

The Mackies looked confused.

'Who the fuck is this cunt?' Wayne said, turning to Dean. 'Is he with you?'

'No, but every time I turn around, the cunt seems to be there.'

'I'm Billy Blackmore.' His voice sounded like ice cracking in a glass. 'And I have something to say.'

'No you don't,' Dean said. He turned to his two thugs. 'I thought I told you twats to give him a message he'd understand.'

The one standing on his own shook his head. 'I think he's brain-damaged or something. He had bandages round his head.'

'Oh yeah,' Dean said. 'What happened to your bandages, dickhead?'

'I need to tell you all something.'

'Billy, stop.' It was Adele.

He turned to her. She had a pleading look on her face.

'It's OK,' he said.

She shook her head. 'You're going to ruin everything. We're getting Ryan back.'

'And I can help.'

'This is a fucking joke,' Wayne said, turning to his gang. 'We're out of here.'

Adele broke free from the thug holding her. 'No, wait. Ignore him. Let's sort this out, I need Ryan back, please. This guy has nothing to do with it.'

Billy walked closer. 'I do.'

Both Dean and Wayne pointed their guns at him.

Adele turned to him. 'Just shut the fuck up,' she said.

He thought he could smell burning. He stopped for a moment, waiting for the flashes in the corner of his eye, the blissful release of a seizure. But nothing happened. He raised a hand and rubbed at his head, making Dean and Wayne focus their guns on him.

Everyone was looking at him, even Ryan. He tried to read what was going through the boy's mind. Billy had never had a dad, his mum never talked about it. But he knew about losing a parent. How old was the boy again, five? What could

Billy remember from when he was five years old? Next to nothing. He hoped Ryan wouldn't remember any of this, would be able to blank it from his mind and live a good and productive life. As much as anyone could.

The burning smell came back to him, a flicker of smoky acidity somewhere at the back of his palate.

Adele turned to stare at Ryan, almost breaking down at the sight of him so close but still unreachable.

Billy looked out beyond Dean and Wayne and the guns pointing at him, at the twinkling of the city, thousands of ordinary people sleeping and dreaming. He wished he were out there with them.

'I killed Frank,' he said.

Adele looked like her face was about to dissolve. 'What did you say?'

He cleared his throat and looked away, couldn't stand to see her eyes on him.

'I said I killed Frank.'

'You must be fucking brain-damaged,' Dean said, stepping closer. 'This is some sick joke, you little shit.'

Billy turned to face Dean, serenity washing over him.

'No joke. I killed your brother. It was an accident.'

'Are you serious?'

Billy nodded. He stepped forward, ignoring the guns pointed at him, and walked between Dean and Wayne. He pointed down to Queen's Drive, to the smattering of trees that lined the road.

'We were driving home from a night out. We hit him. We

thought he was dead. We moved him off the road and drove away.'

'Billy.' It was Adele behind him. 'Look at me.'

He turned and raised his eyes to hers. Her face was full of confusion and hate.

'You killed Frank?'

He tried to speak but couldn't, just nodded.

'All this time, it was you. I can't . . .'

He felt the blow from Dean's gun before he saw it, a heavy thunk of metal on his temple, right about where the bump was, sending familiar bolts of agony through his wrecked body, his fucked mind.

He dropped to his knees and tears came to his eyes.

Dean stood over him, eyes blazing, teeth bared.

'I'm gonna enjoy killing you.' He swung a boot into Billy's stomach. The breath wheezed out of his body along with his spirit, and it felt good to have nothing left in him, nothing left to fight for, just pain and more pain sweeping through him.

He looked up. Adele was watching, tears in her eyes, her hands shaking.

Another blow, this time a kick to his side, a deeper pain than before rocking him as he flinched away from the force of it.

'Jesus fuck.' It was Wayne's voice. 'Look.'

The blows stopped. Billy looked up and Dean was gazing over his head, out over the cliff. Adele was looking the same way. Billy shuffled round slowly to see the flames. He scrunched his eyes tight then opened them again. Still there.

Thick orange flames licking up over the edge of the cliff, only twenty feet away, spreading left and right.

Wayne walked over as far as he could, but the fire had already caught the top of the gorse, and he was pushed back by the heat as thick, flowery smoke billowed upwards into the crystalline sky. He turned back to his brother.

'That was your joint, you dick. You've set fire to the whole fucking hillside.'

Billy's sight was blurry with tears, his eyes now stinging from the smoke. The flames were rampaging through the dry, spindly gorse, weeks of hot weather turning the whole of the Crags into perfect kindling. Reams of smoke rolled over each other as they fought their way into the sky. Billy could feel the heat against his damaged face, searing his skin as he sat hunched over, struggling for breath.

'We've gotta get the fuck out of here,' Wayne said.

'Not until we've got Ryan back.' Dean produced a second handgun. He was pointing one at Wayne, the other straight at Billy. 'And not until I've killed this cunt either.'

'Hey.'

It was a voice from the other direction. The Mackies' third guy. Billy's head swam as he turned and saw Ryan running. It all seemed to slow down, the flickering flames, his little legs moving, Adele reaching towards him, Wayne swinging the shotgun round. He seemed to hesitate as he tracked the small figure with the barrels.

Billy found himself rising, his muscles aching beyond words as he thrust his body forward, a couple of stumbling steps, then he threw himself into Wayne's arm, knocking the shotgun, sending a deafening blast ricocheting around the cliff walls opposite.

Billy felt the judder of a new and terrible pain in his leg, a screaming muscular agony he'd never experienced. He crumpled and fell in a heap on top of Wayne.

Wayne pushed him off. As he rolled, Billy realised the source of the pain, a gaping wound in his thigh, muscle and flesh all ragged and torn, a shy peek of white bone poking out.

'Fuck.'

He clutched at his leg as he lay there, sweat soaking his brow, the roar of the fire and the shotgun blast leaving his ears ringing.

Wayne lunged for the shotgun. But he was too slow. As his fingers reached for the butt of the sawn-off, there were two cracks and his head jerked back in a spray of blood. His body slumped to the ground and he lay motionless.

Billy looked round. Dean still had the gun levelled at Wayne's body. He walked over carefully and slid the shotgun away from Wayne's hand, then kicked the body. Nothing.

Dean looked up and Billy tried to follow his gaze. The pain and tears and smoke were blurring his vision, but he could make out two figures running away. Jamie and the other guy. Jamie had abandoned the crutches and was running with a crazy lolloping stride, the other guy much further away, beginning to disappear in swirls of smoke.

Dean held both of his guns steady and fired twice with each. Jamie jumped then zigzagged sideways, kept running though, not hit. The smoke enveloped him and he was gone.

'Fuck,' Dean said. 'Can't be helped.'

He turned both guns on Billy.

'Seems you've got yourself a little leg wound.'

'Boss.'

It was one of the goons. Dean turned. The guy was pointing down Queen's Drive, beyond the wall of fire and smoke. Flashing lights. The whoop of sirens. Billy couldn't make out if it was fire engines or police.

'We'd better move,' the goon said.

'Not before I finish this cunt off.'

Dean turned back.

The world seemed to shrink.

Smoke caught in Billy's lungs and he coughed, sending blades of pain through his body, from his broken head to his tattered thigh.

Dean lifted both guns and pointed them straight at Billy.

'This is for everything you've done.'

'No.' Adele's voice. Strong and clear.

Dean turned. Adele was standing with the sawn-off shotgun pointing straight at him, Ryan pushed behind her.

Dean smiled. 'What are you doing, darling?'

'This is for everything *you've* done,' she said.

The recoil pushed her backwards as the shotgun went off. In a mirrored movement, Dean was knocked off his feet as the blast ripped through his chest. He staggered backwards for a few steps them slumped to the ground, still gripping a gun in each hand.

Adele dropped the shotgun and turned, pulling Ryan into her body.

The sound of sirens filled the air now. Billy looked round. The two thugs were gone, lumbering down the path. Billy's leg raged with pain. He leaned back and tried to suck in air, his whole body tense with shock.

He lay between the bodies of Dean and Wayne, both still. Adele stared at Dean's body as she held Ryan's hand tight. She looked around. Flashing lights mingled with the flicker of the gorse fire, sirens swooping over the crackle of flames. Smoke seeped through everything.

Adele stared at Billy and he held her gaze.

She looked at Ryan, then down the road.

'Bye, Billy.'

She lifted Ryan up with a heave and began running in the opposite direction from the flashing lights. Billy watched her go, fast and frantic, until she too was swallowed by the smoke.

He gasped and coughed again. It felt like he was in the middle of a funeral pyre. His eyes were foggy, his brain fried. He felt his mind drift as the smoke began to overwhelm him. He closed his eyes.

After a moment he felt something on his face. Wet and rough. A familiar smell. Jeanie. He opened his eyes. She was wagging her tail but looking anxiously at him, pushing at him with her snout. He pulled her close.

'Good girl.'

He tried to push himself up, but collapsed. The pain in his leg was excruciating. He pushed his hands against the dirt and tried to drag himself, but he couldn't. He had nothing left, he was empty.

He slumped to the ground. Jeanie came close and nudged him.

'Go,' he said, his voice broken.

She didn't move.

He gave her a half-hearted shove.

'Go on. Get out of here. If you stay with me you'll die.'

She whined then crept forward to sit next to him.

'Fuck's sake, girl.'

Billy lay on his back. His lungs filled with smoke. His leg was agony, his head too, his body empty. He looked up. Amid the smoke he spotted a sprinkle of stars in the sky. He closed his eyes, felt the soft fur of Jeanie's body alongside. He seemed to drift upwards, beyond everything, growing wings to swoop above the city, diving over the police station and Rankeillor Street, the Whitehouse place and The Crags pub. But his wings caught fire and he tumbled to the ground, thumping into the tarmac of Queen's Drive as Charlie and Zoe looked on.

He heard a voice. Someone calling him. A voice he recognised. From a long time ago. His mum? He listened, straining. He tried so hard to make out who it was, what they were saying. He heard Jeanie's tail thump next to him. Then he felt something else, a hand on his forehead, drawing out all the pain and suffering. He tried to open his eyes but couldn't. He struggled to speak, but just coughed up smoke.

That voice again. He tried to focus. Finally he made something out, from a million miles away, yet right next to him.

'Hold on, Scoop.'

35

The pain felt like an old friend, a part of him he couldn't live without. He couldn't remember a time it hadn't been there.

Click.

The fuzzy glow of morphine, another old compadre, leaching through his body, slipping through the cracks, into his pores, soaking his bones.

He lay for a long time like that, drowning in it.

Then he opened his eyes.

Another hospital ward. Same smells, same light, same washed-out colours.

He couldn't move.

After a while, a nurse spotted his open eyes and came over. He looked at a glass of water on the bedside table. She lifted it to his lips and he sipped. Cold and shocking. He choked, his brain throbbing in time.

The nurse reassured him, then left.

He closed his eyes and lay still. He didn't know how long for.

Eventually he was aware of someone nearby. He opened his eyes.

He tried to smile but it hurt too much.

She eased herself on to the bed. 'Take it easy, Scoop.'

She took his hand. A drip was feeding into it.

He tried to speak but could only croak.

'It's OK.' She patted his hand. 'You've been unconscious for two days, just relax, there's no hurry.'

Billy tried to push himself up on to his elbows but couldn't.

'How?' he whispered.

Rose smiled. 'True crime reporter, Scoop, always wanting to know the hows and whys, eh?'

Billy's body felt like a lead casket at the bottom of the ocean.

'Not much to fill in,' Rose said. 'I got your message just after you left it. The phone ringing woke me up. I tried to call you back but your phone was off. I called DI Price then headed round to the Crags. Arrived just before the police. By the time I got there it was carnage. You injured, Lassie by your side, two dead bodies and a hillside on fire. Very dramatic. Made for a fantastic front page, I can tell you.'

Billy felt Rose's fingers warm against his limp hand.

'In fact, the *Standard* has been full of your exploits. We pieced everything together from your message and various police interviews. Stuart has kept me abreast of those. Adele Whitehouse and Jamie Mackie, your brother and Zoe.'

She gave Billy a look.

'Adele says that Wayne Mackie and Dean Whitehouse shot each other, and you got caught in the crossfire. That right?'

Billy pictured Adele holding the shotgun, the look on her face.

He nodded.

Rose raised her eyebrows.

'Charlie and Zoe have been suspended from the hospital and paper respectively. I wouldn't recommend going back to Rankeillor Street any time soon. I would say come and stay with me, but by the time you're fit to get out of here, I suspect the police will have other plans for you.'

Billy nodded again. 'Jeanie?'

'The faithful hound is at my place. I can look after her until . . . well, until you're better.' She got up. 'The police are waiting to talk to you. I charmed my way in first for two minutes, wanted to check you were OK.'

Billy put on a weak smile. 'Never better.'

'That's my boy, Scoop.'

She leaned in and gave him a gentle kiss on the forehead. His head had been re-bandaged. He caught her perfume, that sticky, flowery scent, like gorse blossom.

She put her hands on her hips. 'You should've told me, you know. About Frank.'

'I know.'

She walked away. At the doorway, she stopped and waved, then she was gone.

In her wake, DI Price and another officer came in.

Billy watched as they walked towards his bed.

He sank into his pillows and felt relieved for the first time in as long as he could remember.

An Interview with Doug Johnstone

Hit and Run opens with a memorably nasty accident, a hit and run no less. It's not the first time a car accident has shown up in your work, what's the fascination?

I wish I could explain it, but I can't really. I am obsessed with car crashes of all kinds, although I think I might have finally got it out of my system with this novel. Before *Hit and Run* I wrote several stories containing car crashes, it was the pivotal moment in *Smokeheads*, and I also wrote a couple of short film scripts and a handful of songs about them as well. I did crash my parents' car when I was 18, but that was a lifetime ago, so no idea why it's wriggled to the surface now. I found the central premise of *Hit and Run* compelling though – what would you do in that situation? OK, you've been stupid, but it was an accident, and that idea about a split-second decision irrevocably changing your life from that moment on is fascinating. Car crashes are, by their nature, hugely dramatic events, something that makes them ideal for fiction, and they happen all the time all around us, they're so commonplace we kind of ignore them, something I find very weird indeed.

Can you say a little about the Radical Road where the accident takes place?

The accident actually happens on Queen's Drive, just below the Radical Road, which is a path that runs round the side of Salisbury Crags, the steep cliffs that run from Arthur's Seat down to Holyrood Park in the centre of Edinburgh. The road gets its name because it was paved in the nineteenth century in the aftermath of the Radical War of 1820, a week of strikes and civil unrest. As a student, I lived in the shadow of the Crags for many years, and it always struck me as a very dramatic backdrop – I always thought it was mad that a few minutes' walk from the centre of our capital city you had cliffs and mountains and grasslands that feel like you're in the middle of nowhere. The part the Radical Road plays in *Hit and Run* is crucial, the whole of the Crags acting as a focus for the action, looming over everything. There's a sense of danger up there as well, it would be very easy just to step off the path and plunge 100 feet to your death – in fact a teenage boy was found dead at the bottom recently after accidentally falling off.

And following on from that, Edinburgh itself is powerfully evoked, almost a character in its own right. Was that a conscious decision from the start, or something that emerged as you wrote it?

I always attempt to create a strong sense of place in my fiction – whether I succeed or not is up to the reader, I guess. But it was very definitely part of the plan – to portray the landscape and psyche of the city I've lived in for over twenty years. Edinburgh is, of course, a very familiar landscape in fiction, especially in crime fiction, but I still felt I had something to add. When I first started writing novels, I shied away from depicting Edinburgh a little, but for this book I decided it was time for me to carve out the place for myself. Almost all the action happens in the city's Southside and Newington neighbourhoods – not necessarily the touristy parts that most people know, and not the Leith of Irvine Welsh, but something different, an area I knew like the back of my hand for a long time and that has its own distinct personality. I'm not really sure what the trick is to portraying that sense of place, though, although I seem to be OK at it – it's certainly one of the things that reviewers and readers pick up on, so hopefully I can keep it up.

You said somewhere while promoting *Smokeheads*, your previous novel, that you wanted to write a short, sharp, shock of a novel, a piece of fiction with 'no fat'. If anything, you've taken that edict even further this time. Again, was that something you set out to do?

Yes, absolutely. I've had my eyes opened over the last few years by reading a lot of the classic noir canon – Jim Thompson, James M. Cain and all that – and it's had a massive effect on me as a writer. I just find real beauty in the most stripped-down language possible – there is a subtle elegance in portraying ideas, scenes, characters and dialogue in as clinically concise a way as possible. I find it incredibly hard to read flabby or verbose writing now; it irritates me beyond belief. Any kind of writing that draws attention to itself – 'Look at me! The terribly clever author!' – makes me want to puke.

The two novels do seem to make a pair, stylistically at least, with this clipped, noirish style, which you set brilliantly against contemporary Scottish landscapes. Are there any particular writers or novels that influenced this approach for you?

In terms of subject matter or setting, not really, but in terms of style there were a few of those classic noir stories that blew me away. James M. Cain's *Double Indemnity* is just a masterclass in clear writing, while Horace McCoy's *They Shoot Horses, Don't They?* and Nathanael West's *Miss Lonely-hearts* are crazy, subversive tales that manage to pack an almighty punch in under a hundred pages each.

Going back to *Smokeheads*, you set the whole novel on the island of Islay, which was a brilliant move, dramatically, and also of course gave you the hook of single malt whiskies. I wondered when the ideas for that novel first started to all come together for you?

Well there were a couple of starting points really, which kind of meshed together. I've long been a fan of James Dickey's novel *Deliverance*, which I came to from the classic Burt

Reynolds movie. I loved the contained tension created by the physical constraints on the action, and I thought that doing something similar on a Scottish island would be interesting. I've been a big fan of single malt whiskies for many years, specifically Islay ones, which have a very distinct style and personality. It struck me that you could have a kind of buddy movie thing similar to *Sideways* by Rex Pickett with whisky instead of wine, then flick a switch and turn it into *Deliverance* crossed with *The Wicker Man*. OK, that doesn't exactly sound like rocket science or great art, but hopefully what I've created has some kind of merit, at least as a decent piece of storytelling.

You're also an experienced musician; I wondered what you saw as the similarities and differences between songwriting and novel writing?

For me, songwriting is a lot more instinctive than novel writing. Of course, there is still a creative element to each, but a novel takes so much more planning – at least the way I do it. I write huge amounts of notes in preparation for writing a novel, as well as character profiles, scene sketches, loads of stuff, and then when I'm brimming over with material, I kind of just splurge it onto the page. The songs seem to come in a much less planned way, much more of a scattershot approach. You really can write a song in five minutes if you're in the right mood, and often those are much better than the ones you slave away over for ages and spend weeks crafting and re-shaping.

Looking ahead, what's next, fiction-wise?

I'm working on the next novel, which I think will fit in stylistically with *Smokeheads* and *Hit and Run*, while hopefully having deeper psychology behind it and a wider social commentary. I don't want to say too much about it at the moment, but it's set in Edinburgh again, this time mostly in the area around Portobello beach, where I now live. It's about a man whose wife goes missing, leaving him to look after their young son while also following the trail of her disappearance, a trail that unravels into something of a nightmare situation. It's the most disturbing subject matter I've tackled so if I can pull it off, it'll hopefully make for a powerful read.

And finally, rapid-fire round, it's time for some of Doug Johnstone's recommendations:

Favourite novel?

Preston Falls by the massively underrated David Gates.

Favourite album?

Probably *Vivadixiesubmarinetransmissionplot,* the first Sparklehorse album.

Favourite single malt whisky?

Obvious, given the context of *Smokeheads*, but it has to be Laphroaig.

ff

Faber and Faber is one of the great independent publishing houses. We were established in 1929 by Geoffrey Faber with T. S. Eliot as one of our first editors. We are proud to publish award-winning fiction and non-fiction, as well as an unrivalled list of poets and playwrights. Among our list of writers we have five Booker Prize winners and twelve Nobel Laureates, and we continue to seek out the most exciting and innovative writers at work today.

Find out more about our authors and books
faber.co.uk

Read our blog for insight and opinion on books and the arts
thethoughtfox.co.uk

Follow news and conversation
twitter.com/faberbooks

Watch readings and interviews
youtube.com/faberandfaber

Connect with other readers
facebook.com/faberandfaber

Explore our archive
flickr.com/faberandfaber